Wisconsin Indianhead Technical Institute
2100 Beaser
Ashland, WI 54806

A Candlelight Ecstasy Romance®

"DID YOU ENJOY DOING THAT? DID YOU?"
HE STEPPED CLOSER TO HER.

"Oh, please, why the look of confusion? You weren't confused when you talked to the press, when you posed for pictures. You enjoyed being the hero, didn't you, Cam? Wowing everyone with your kung fu prowess." Then suddenly Thor's eyes narrowed. "What are you staring at?"

"Not much."

"What kind of crack is that?"

"The truth. Apparently, I had a better opinion of you than you deserve," Cam said.

"What's that supposed to mean?"

"It means I thought I'd finally found a man who was not interested in a clichéd woman. I don't need a man to make me feel like something, or to be controlled. I can walk, talk, think, act, love—without asking permission. All women can. Most women do."

CANDLELIGHT ECSTASY CLASSIC ROMANCES

CANDLELIGHT ECSTASY ROMANCES®

QUANTITY SALES

Most Dell Books are available at special quantity discounts when purchased in bulk by corporations, organizations, and special-interest groups. Custom imprinting or excerpting can also be done to fit special needs. For details write: Dell Publishing Co., Inc., 1 Dag Hammarskjold Plaza, New York, NY 10017, Attn.: Special Sales Dept., or phone: (212) 605-3319.

INDIVIDUAL SALES

Are there any Dell Books you want but cannot find in your local stores? If so, you can order them directly from us. You can get any Dell book in print. Simply include the book's title, author, and ISBN number, if you have it, along with a check or money order (no cash can be accepted) for the full retail price plus 75¢ per copy to cover shipping and handling. Mail to: Dell Readers Service, Dept. FM, 6 Regent Street, Livingston, N.J. 07039.

Wisconsin Indianhead Technical Institute
2100 Beaser
Ashland, WI 54806

DARE
THE DEVIL

Elaine Raco Chase

A CANDLELIGHT ECSTASY ROMANCE®

Published by
Dell Publishing Co., Inc.
1 Dag Hammarskjold Plaza
New York, New York 10017

Copyright © 1987 by Elaine Raco Chase

All rights reserved. No part of this book may be reproduced or transmitted in any form or by any means, electronic or mechanical, including photocopying, recording or by any information storage and retrieval system, without the written permission of the Publisher, except where permitted by law.

Dell ® TM 681510, Dell Publishing Co., Inc.

Candlelight Ecstasy Romance®, 1,203,540, is a registered trademark of Dell Publishing Co., Inc., New York, New York.

ISBN: 0-440-11759-3

Printed in the United States of America

April 1987

10 9 8 7 6 5 4 3 2 1

WFH

Wisconsin Indianhead Technical Institute
2100 Beaser
Ashland, WI 54806

This is the first novel written after I was in a severe auto accident. It would have never been completed except for a SEAT BELT.

I value all my friends and readers too much not to share that information. If you want to add something to your life, make it the security and protection of a seat belt/shoulder harness—back seat or front—especially when it comes to your children.

A special note of thanks to Lydia Paglio and Dell Publishing for their patience (above and beyond), understanding, and support.

To Our Readers:

We have been delighted with your enthusiastic response to Candlelight Ecstasy Romances®, and we thank you for the interest you have shown in this exciting series.

In the upcoming months we will continue to present the distinctive sensuous love stories you have come to expect only from Ecstasy. We look forward to bringing you many more books from your favorite authors and also the very finest work from new authors of contemporary romantic fiction.

As always, we are striving to present the unique, absorbing love stories that you enjoy most—books that are more than ordinary romance. Your suggestions and comments are always welcome. Please write to us at the address below.

Sincerely,

The Editors
Candlelight Romances
1 Dag Hammarskjold Plaza
New York, New York 10017

DARE
THE DEVIL

CHAPTER ONE

"I found 'em! I found 'em!" The youthful rider reigned his pony so sharply that the brown and white pinto reared and made the other horses skitter sideways, snorting uneasily. "Wait'll you see—you won't believe —but it's true—it's real." The boy's words became tangled by his excitement. "Crazy but real. They're there. I saw them." He held up his palm. "Honest."

"Take it easy, son," commanded a husky, authoritative voice. "Here, cool down with this." A canteen was passed by twelve pairs of hands until it reached its mark. "Billy, you shouldn't have gone off on your own. We were just about to turn ourselves into a search party."

Blue eyes watched in silent amusement while the thirteen-year-old's face went through animated changes as he guzzled the canteen water with hearty abandon, finishing with a loud burp.

Billy Campbell wiped the back of his hand across his mouth, mixing a dribble of water with dust that smeared a dirty path over freckled cheeks. "I—I'm sorry, Mr. Devlin, but," he gulped, "wait till you hear what I found."

"Just what did you find?"

"Tracks." Billy yelped. "Big tracks. Biggest things I've ever seen."

"I knew it, Thor," Nate Garvin interjected. "Those damn rustlers are usin' trucks to steal the cattle." He yanked down the brim on the sweat-stained raffia straw hat to further shade his eyes from the bright July sun. "Probably an eighteen-wheeler. Describe what you saw, boy."

"Not *tire* tracks," Billy told the foreman. "Animal, Nate. Funny ones. Like this." His arms formed a circle. "Cat tracks too. Big. Real big."

"Stop exaggeratin' boy," Nate demanded over the excited whispers of the two other teenagers who were riding with the wranglers. Saddle leather creaked under his lean weight as he turned to his boss. "What the hell was in your canteen, Thor?"

"Spring water."

"I knew you wouldn't believe me!" Billy's plaintive falsetto sliced through the chatter. Taking a deep breath, the teenager sat taller in the saddle. "Well, I saw more than just tracks," he added stubbornly. "I heard—"

"And just what did you hear, boy?" Nate spat a stream of tobacco juice at an untrampled anthill.

Billy's gaze didn't waver. "Snarling. Lots of snarling and . . . trumpeting."

"Snarlin' and trumpetin'?" The foreman gave a loud hoot that was echoed by the ranch hands. He closed one brown eye, and stared with cold contemplation at the surly youth with the other. "Say, didn't you boys stay up late last night watchin' horror movies on Thor's vid-e-o machine? I say your 'magination's workin' overtime. Maybe you had a . . . daymare."

"This wasn't my imagination or a daymare either." Billy shifted his gaze to Thor. "I—I saw one of 'em, Mr. Devlin." His dark eyes seemed to double in size, dominating his small face. "It was big. Big as a mountain.

12

Covered with fur and tusks. Tusks long as a fence rail. It—it was . . . pre—prehysterical!"

Thor studied the youth for a moment, then cleared his throat. "All right, Billy Campbell, lead on to this *prehistorical* find."

"Yes, sir!" Wheeling the pony left, Billy let out a war cry that he hoped would echo the twenty-two miles over the Continental Divide to the Blackfeet Indian Reservation.

Forty-eight hooves thundered a path through the prairie grasses, trampling the pasqueflowers and slashing the blossoms on the yellow bells. The riders did not temper their heat-lathered horses until the towering aspen grew too thick in the groves to allow any speed.

"The clearing's comin' up," a breathless Billy yelled. "That's where I first spotted all the tracks. I saw the—the beast at the base of the escarpment."

Thor's hand signal halted the riders at the edge of the coppice. "Maybe we better take a long-distance look-see at your beast." He reached into his saddlebag for binoculars.

Nate shook his head. "Beast, yuh? I'll be damned if I don't think your 'magination is runnin' like the boy's."

"It goes with the territory," came his boss's grinning pronouncement. "Time seems to stand still here. Glacier Country has peaks so steep and remote they've never been climbed and contains virtually every predator and prey species since the Ice Age."

The foreman emitted a disgusted snort. "Yeah, but you don't actually believe that Billy saw a—a . . ."

"Stranger things, Nate." His voice was oddly noncommittal. Thor focused on the vast eminence of jagged limestone mountains. The formidable landscape never failed to hold him in awe of Nature's freezing hand that aeons ago carved cirques, shaved peaks, and moved

13

mountains. "I haven't been in this area since I was a kid."

He stared at the tortuous escarpment. The dark, steep cliffs, gnarled precipices, and craggy summit haunted an otherwise sunny azure sky. The prevailing atmosphere on this pocket of ranch land was different. Disquieting. Eerie. Primeval. Prehistoric.

A childhood memory stirred within Thor Devlin's brain. A long forgotten door slowly creaked open and released a ghost. He tried to shake off the mood but failed. It had been here, in this savage-looking place, where, at the age of thirteen, he had met a *beast*.

A *beast* that had attacked without provocation. Eight feet, eight hundred pounds of rogue black grizzly. Thor had lost his horse and nearly his life to the animal and for a long time, both day and night, fear became his constant companion. His thumb and forefinger massaged away beads of sweat that dampened his thick mustache.

"Godforsaken place," Nate muttered, his body feeling chilled despite the heat. "Hell, there ain't nothin' here." He added, "I've been foreman for forty-five years and ain't never crossed this way. No need to. Cattle don't stray here. Nor horses." His head hunched between raised, protective shoulders. "Nothin' but rocks and sky. Maybe a few mountain goats. But I'll bet a week's pay that there ain't no beast. Probably just an oversized goat!"

"I'll take that bet," Billy snapped. "Because I know what I saw and—"

A groaning bellow erupted, an indescribable, continuous confusion of sound that shook the towering pines and sent rocks and sand drizzling from the crags.

Suddenly silent riders tried to stabilize their excited horses.

"There! I told you!" came the teenager's gleeful

14

chorus. Then Billy sobered. "You don't suppose that's a cry of hunger?"

"Don't worry. We're not here to be anything's lunch." Thor looped the unused binoculars around the saddle horn and reached to check the bullets in the breech of the .357 Magnum holstered at his waist. "Boys, I want you at least six feet behind the last man." His voice was a cool assumption of command that eliminated any further comments. "Let's go. Quietly. Carefully." His boot heels cued the stallion into a cautious walk.

Aspen, pine, and fir became less and less. Thor took silent note of the unusual rutted tracks in the clearing. Then the landscape again yielded to the limestone rocks and twisted-trunked evergreens that seemingly grew out of a thick foggy blanket.

Thor stared at the tumbled and warped architecture of deathbed colors that surrounded him. "This isn't right," came his thoughtful murmur. "The land couldn't have changed this much. And this thick mist. No, this definitely is not right. Nate, I—" Thor stuttered into silence when visibility abruptly increased. There, in the distance, his eyes locked onto Billy's beast.

The first whispered words that tumbled from Nate's lips were more prayer than blasphemy. "What in hell is that?"

"Mammoth. A woolly mammoth." Thor's low tone echoed the expression of disbelief that settled on his face.

"Look at the size of that thing," muttered five wranglers in unison. "What d'ya guess, boss?"

"Fourteen feet. Four tons. Plus the tusks. Those curved pieces of ivory look to be a good twelve feet."

Twenty-four eyes widened in further amazement watching as the huge, dark gray, fur-covered mammoth proceeded to use his head as a battering ram to topple a twenty-foot aspen. The bull's stomach rumbled noisily all the while his six-foot trunk calmly began to strip the branches and place them in his mouth.

"Where in hell did it come from?" Nate hissed.

"Billy's beast is set to celebrate his ten thousandth birthday," Thor countered, laying a calming hand against his horse's neck. "Steady there, boy. I—"

"Boss! Look up there!" Buck Taylor's undertone crackled with excitement as he pointed two hundred yards up at the limestone precipice. "That cat! Those—those teeth!"

Scrambling for the binoculars, Thor raised them for a closer look. "I'll be damned." He turned to Nate. "That's a saber-toothed tiger."

"Saber-toothed?" The foreman grabbed for the glasses. "If you're funnin' me, Thor, I'll . . ." Nate's Adam's apple bobbed in amazement. "Holy sh—! I ain't never seen a cat that size. Must be," he licked his lips and adjusted the focus for a sharper image, "four hundred pounds. And look at those curved canines!"

Thor's blue eyes narrowed in critical evaluation of all they had seen. "Something just doesn't wash here. First the knee-deep fog, then the woolly mammoth, now we've got a forty-million-year-old saber-toothed cat. I just don't buy that we've stumbled into a time warp."

Nate suddenly strangled on his tobacco juice. "I'll be double damned. What about *her?* What about the *naked female savage* up there with the tiger!"

A forceful yank brought the binoculars back to Thor's eyes.

If the sun and too much lunch hadn't rendered her heavy with sleep, she would have heard them sooner. Now it was too late. A dozen men, horses in tow, had already mounted the precipice, cutting off any escape.

She had no place to run.

Her only alternative was to stand her ground and wait until the rest of her group returned. They couldn't be too much longer. Hell, they were already two hours overdue. All she had to do was stall and she did have an edge. The fingers of her right hand locked around the thong collar that circled the big cat's muscular neck.

Smiling slightly and listening to her powerful companion purr, she doubted any of these men had nerve enough to get too close. But if they tried, she had a few tricks up her sleeve. She knew exactly what to say and do to make the tawny feline go from purring cat to snarling tiger.

The men were now only twenty feet away. A silent battle ensued. She stared at them. They stared at her. Astonishment, incredulity, and intrigue chased themselves over assorted sun-bronzed masculine faces.

She decided to play dumb. Let them make the first move. Perhaps keep them guessing, keep them wondering, keep them off-balance—just until the others arrived.

Her inherent sense of self-preservation and survival took over. She judged each man individually, assessing her own odds. The three teenage boys were quickly dismissed. Her eyes gauged the others. They varied in age from mid-twenties to sixties. Bodies matched faces— tough and strong, courtesy of hard, physical labor. She knew she could physically disable six of the wranglers rather quickly.

Her gaze shifted to the man leading a wild-eyed buckskin stallion. Despite the fact that no one had violated the silence, she did not doubt that he was the boss. While the black hat he was wearing cast a shadow on his face, she easily recognized an unmistakable air of self-confidence and authority. It showed in his powerful build, in his walk and his impressive carriage.

And if such nicely packaged masculine charms had

17

been displayed in any other place and under any other circumstances, she would have been the first one to show appropriate feminine appreciation. But this was not the right time or the right place.

She did, however, notice a subtle change in a few of the younger cowboys. It was her fault, she quickly acknowledged. The silence had gone on too long. While she had been assessing them, they had been assessing her. Caution and disbelief had been replaced by that old macho hormonal curse, lust.

When she saw leers slant a half-dozen lips, her thumb and forefinger pressed into the cat's neck. His wide-mouthed, fanged snarl immediately sent the horses into hysterics and restored more respectful expressions on the mens' faces.

Her victory, however, was brief. One minute later she heard the distinct snap of a bolt-action repeating rifle and found three of them aimed at the cat and a fourth at her.

"Hold it, boys." Thor stepped between the guns and their targets. "Let's keep calm. Buck, pull the horses way back. All right, relax, everybody. There's no need to get trigger happy."

"Maybe she doesn't understand English, Thor," Nate piped, observing her moccasins. "Let me try some Blackfeet." He cleared his throat and offered, *"Kokipi sni menuah."*

Thor exhaled a painful groan and turned to look at the foreman. "Nate! I don't think 'do not fear, let's take a bath' is very appropriate!"

With one eye on the men, she lowered her chin and tried hard to control the laughter that threatened to bubble forth. Her left hand made a graceful gesture that shielded her smile and then moved on to straighten the bear-claw necklace at her throat.

The instant the man called Thor advanced two more

steps toward her, she stiffened in wary attention. Fingers tightened on the cat's leather collar, her left hand dropping against the ivory handle of the knife sheathed in her loincloth.

Suddenly, Thor found himself facing two predators. He didn't miss the lethal quality in her taut, ready-for-combat stance. Neither had the saber-toothed cat. A growl rolled in his throat; powerful haunches were tensed for attack.

Still, the closer he got, the more certain he became that all was not what it appeared to be. "Seems we've got a Mexican standoff here." His deep voice was calm as he used slow and careful movements to take off his hat. "No one has to get hurt."

Thor knew she could understand every word. The animals appeared prehistoric but the lady certainly wasn't. She was, Thor decided, a rather haute couture savage. Little concessions to feminine accoutrements gave her away, like the scent of skillfully blended perfume that drifted on the breeze and the mauve tinting that glossed her full lips. And then there was her hair—a tawny mix of platinum and gold waves, curls, and precision-cut layers that swirled in elegant dishevelment around her bare shoulders.

While she wasn't naked, her wearing apparel left little to the imagination. High, rounded breasts were individually encased in chamois triangles hooked together by leather strips; the same laces secured a loincloth that bared sinuous thighs and sleek hips.

His gaze lingered an appreciative extra minute on her bronzed, supple body and then returned to study her face. Thor was surprised to find how easy he became a prisoner of her eyes, eloquent eyes that were soft and full of character and intelligence. Almond shaped, slightly slanted, with dark blue irises, they were made

19

mysterious by a fringe of jet lashes that looked natural despite the obvious contrast with her leonine coloring.

He liked the confident way she held her head and how the sun-gold curls that tumbled onto her forehead defied the leather headband. There was a roundness about her face that was soft, inviting, and he instinctively knew that his little finger would fit perfectly in the cleft of her chin.

Surprised at harboring such an intimate thought, Thor took a step back but his gaze was locked onto hers. "I'd really appreciate an explanation of all this. You, the hairy elephant, and the cat with the overbite are not the norm in Montana. So anytime you'd like to begin . . ."

She really wished he had never spoken. The deep, husky whisper of his voice caused her breath to quicken. She also wished he hadn't removed his hat. Now that his features were readily visible, she found agreeable sensations flooding her veins.

He had a head like a Norse god. Thick brown-blond curly hair brushed up and back from his face. A face weathered by experience. A nice face. A very, very nice face, she mentally corrected.

His physical features were both strong and gentle. Wide-set ice-blue eyes, large cheekbones, small nose, and a fierce chin and jawline. She had always been a sucker for a mustache and his grew thick and brown over a sensuous top lip.

He had a body that was impossible to ignore, so she gave up trying. Her gaze wandered up and down a six-foot-plus physique that was the epitome of strength and vigor, displayed to full advantage in jeans and a denim shirt, the sleeves rolled up to his midarm. The leather gun holster that slung low on his lean hips gave him an aura of danger that she found rather enticing.

Her relaxed appraisal hadn't gone unnoticed by either the man or the large cat. The latter proved to be her undoing. His mouth opened not to snarl but to emit a long, loud, kittenish yawn. The tiger rolled over, rubbed his back and shoulders into the ground, his hind legs spread-eagled, yawned again, and pawed sleepily at his face. To the amazement of everyone, his swordlike canine teeth fell out.

"Damn it, Pumpkin, why couldn't you have just growled!"

"Pumpkin?" Thor blinked. "Pumpkin!" Ragged, sun-bleached eyebrows drew together. "That cat's name is—"

"Pumpkin," she supplied, her mouth tilting with humor. "By the way, the hairy elephant is just that."

"I suppose his name is Jumbo?"

"No, Ramon." Her eyes grew bright and, after placing two fingers between her lips, let loose with an ear-splitting whistle. The furry pachyderm responded with an equally deafening wail that sent the horses into a frenzy.

Thor crossed his arms over his chest and took a deep breath. "Well, that gives two out of three names. What about you?"

"Cam Stirling," she extended her hand. "You are Thor—"

"Luthor Devlin." He wasn't quite sure why he formalized his name, except the childhood nickname seemed too frivolous to say to a woman with such a firm grip.

She studied him for a long moment, liking a little too much what she saw. "I think Thor fits you so much better." Her eyelid lowered in a slow wink. "The reigning god of thunder and lightning, the ruler of the sky and this is *Big Sky* country."

Realizing he was still holding her hand, Thor released

it, cleared his throat, and tried to establish a more serious vein of conversation. "I'd like some answers."

"I'll just bet you have some great questions." Abruptly, Cam realized that there were more than just two people on the limestone cliff. She watched the other men move closer and raised her voice. "There isn't any need for those rifles." Her posture became defensive. "My friend is quite gentle." To prove her point, she dropped to her knees, rubbed the big cat's massive chest until he began to purr, then playfully tweaked his nose.

"What in hell's goin' on here?" Nate demanded, shoving through the muttering queue. He squinted at the utterly relaxed, obviously contented animal. "Why, he's nothin' but a goll dang pussycat!"

Cam smiled at the foreman. "He's an overgrown cougar but with the help of a good set of dentures," she opened the animal's massive jaw and replaced the foot-long canines, "and a snarl that he's been practicing for three months, Pumpkin's a saber-toothed tiger." She stood up in one graceful movement. "All it takes is magic."

"Magic?" Nate scratched his stubbled jaw. "Why and what for?"

"Movie magic," came Thor's calm interjection.

Turning her head, Cam discovered he'd moved close to her side. "That's right. Both of my friends are movie stars. As a matter of fact, I'm sure you've seen Pumpkin in quite a few TV commercials and on billboards. He sells suntan lotion and cars."

"Is all this for one of them TeeVee commercials?" the lanky foreman inquired.

She shook her head. "No, we're—"

"Movies." Billy blurted. "I bet you're here making a movie. Are you the star?"

"Yes and no." Before she could explain further, another new sound assaulted the group's ears. The whirling single rotor blade of a helicopter walloped the air. As the chopper hovered over the escarpment, the winds from the wing sent dirt and gravel upward off the ground and made the horses go wild in fright. Cam immediately raised her hand in an all clear signal, then motioned the pilot toward the clearing.

She turned toward Luthor Devlin and did something she had wanted to do from the first moment—touch him. "Your poor horses have had quite a scare today." Her left hand settled comfortably on his right forearm; his taut flesh was warm and very masculine.

Thor looked from her hand to her eyes. "It's been an interesting day all around." He made no attempt to liberate his arm. Instead, he found pleasure in her touch. "I'm still a little confused as to what's going on here."

Cam reacted with surprise. "The memo that went out from your forest supervisor was quite clear."

"Memo?"

"Yes, to all the rangers. We do have the proper permits and I know Jack is giving credit to the Glacier National Park at the end of his film."

"I hate sounding like an echo," Thor responded evenly, "but who is Jack?"

"Jack Kenyon, Kenyon Productions." She gave an encouraging little smile. "He won three Oscars last year for his sci-fi epic."

Thor shook his head, then grinned at her musical sigh.

"Perhaps Bridget Lawson might ring a few bells."

"Bridget Lawson . . . hmm . . . if I'm not mistaken there are at least three of her posters hanging in the bunkhouse."

"How nice to discover that your men are art lovers!"

"What can I tell you," came his lazy rejoinder. Thor patted her hand and then left his on top of hers. "She's nailed right up there next to all the Monets and Picassos."

Cam took a step closer, her feet straddling one heavily scuffed brown boot. "Well, Bridget is the star of Jack's latest movie and by the enthusiastic sounds coming from your cowboys, she and Kenyon must have stepped into full view." Looking over his shoulder, she waved at four new arrivals and shouted, "I'll be right down."

Thor's hand caught and held her wrist. He didn't like her breaking contact. "So, you're not the star?"

Her blond hair whipped back and forth across her bare shoulders. "Nope. She's the star." Cam was surprised when he still didn't turn around. Surprised and pleased.

"And you?"

"I'm the action technician." She saw his right eyebrow rise and sighed. "Stunt woman."

"What's the name of this little epic?"

"Empress of Armageddon." Tapping his fingers free of her hand, Cam called the cat to attention by her side. "Now, I really must report to my boss." Her soft eyes grew lustrous. "I'll introduce you after you make the long—" she lengthened the word, "climb down."

Seconds later, Thor and his ranch hands watched in rapt fascination as Cam Stirling did anything but laboriously *climb* down the rugged face of the escarpment. What had taken the men at least a dozen panting, sweat-laden minutes, she accomplished in less than five. It was as if there were no jagged limestone folds or scoured rock surfaces.

She duplicated the cat, not just in coloring but in sinuous grace. Cam traveled fluid-smooth and nimble down the steep, stratified slopes. Her movements were agile and lithe and possessed the style and elegance of a prima ballerina.

"She's as sure a' foot as a mountain goat," Nate commented, putting a fresh chaw of tobacco into his mouth.

Thor hadn't realized how long he'd been holding his breath until he tried to speak and found himself gasping. He swallowed hard. "More like a gazelle."

Nate expelled a thin stream of tobacco juice. "So, what d'ya think?"

"I'm trying not to." With that insouciant comment, he pulled his hat brim low on his forehead, grabbed his horse's reins, and slowly, carefully headed down the rock-strewn crag.

Jack quickly scratched out another notation—replenish the fog—before snapping his producer's logbook closed. "Very, very nice, Cam, but you should have saved all that graceful energy for when the cameras roll." He looked beyond her to the parade of men and horses maneuvering slowly down the cliff. "Don't tell me a ranger brought a tourist group over for the afternoon. Dammit, we don't have time to nursemaid visitors. Hell's bells, can't anyone read—"

Cam placed a restraining hand on his shoulder. "They didn't know a thing about the memo, Jack. Apparently, they were out riding, blundered right in, and got the shock of their lives seeing Pumpkin and Ramon." She patted and praised the big cat, then smiled at the blond actress who had moved to join the producer. "Your poster seems to be quite popular with those men, Bridget."

"At least they have excellent taste!" Bridget Lawson lowered oversized sunglasses to peer at the encroaching group. "Let's not be rude to an adoring public, Jack. After all, they're the ones who'll be spending the money to see me in your latest."

Jack took off his Pirates' baseball cap, used a handkerchief to blot the sweat from his bald head and bushy black beard, then took a deep breath. "Okay, ladies, let's go make nice-nice with the crowd and then walk through the new changes while we wait for the three other choppers to bring the cast, crew, and equipment."

After leaving the cat with his trainer for some makeup repairs and water, Cam made the necessary introductions. "Jack Kenyon, Bridget Lawson, this is Luthor Devlin."

The two men shook hands, sizing each other up in that brief moment. Jack had to crane his neck an extra eight inches to look Thor in the eyes. "Cam told me how you stumbled onto our set and—"

"We'd love to have you stay and watch our afternoon shooting," Bridget Lawson inserted smoothly, her coquettish nature surging to the surface at Thor's handsome face.

His gaze shifted to locate Cam Stirling. She had settled quite comfortably on a nearby boulder, one shapely leg swinging in time to silent music, her mouth tilted in a smile. Thor's gaze again returned to Bridget Lawson. At first glance, the two women could indeed pass for identical twins but to Thor's eyes the differences were highly pronounced.

Bridget Lawson's style was dramatic and affected, her sexuality so pouty and overt that she came off as a comic-strip cutie rather than a sensual woman. Sensual woman. Once again Thor found himself drawn to Cam Stirling. She was earthy, natural, strong, and slightly cocky. He liked that. Liked that a little too damn much!

Nate moved to his boss's side. "So, you're the star, are ya'," he eyed Bridget's buxom form. "You look healthy enough. Why ain't you doin' your own runnin'?"

Bridget inspected the lanky foreman with all the discipline of a scientist examining a laboratory animal. She mentally deemed his appearance as slovenly and pronounced him unimportant. Her manner became icy. "Insurance. I'm just too valuable to the production company. They use stunt people for the more physical tasks. They can be replaced. If I'm injured, this picture shuts down and people are out of work."

The foreman's only comment was to jettison yellow-brown tobacco juice at a nearby scrub bush.

"Really!" Bridget moved a step behind Jack and stage whispered, "Perhaps we should pick and choose who gets to stay. As I remember I do have the final say, and I say this is a closed set."

"I'm not sure *I'll* allow any of you to stay," came Thor's equally caustic response.

"You'll allow! What the hell do you mean *you'll* allow?" Jack pulled a folded piece of paper from the pocket of his tan Bermuda shorts. "Listen, buddy, you'd better put in a call to your supervisor. We're cleared and approved. I've got all the necessary permits needed to shoot a movie on federal government property."

Thor reached for the paper, crumbled it in his massive fist, and threw it on the ground.

"Hey!" Jack yelped. "You can't do that! You can't—"

"The hell I can't. This isn't United States Forest Service property. This is Devlin land."

CHAPTER TWO

If she was forced to swallow one more laugh, Cam knew she'd choke to death. Inhaling a deep sobering breath, she conformed her body to the sun-warmed, red-lichened boulder and played silent spectator to a scene that was more hilarious than any scripted comedy. Her mouth tried, albeit unsuccessfully, to keep from grinning as she watched a yapping terrier and a yipping Pekingese go up against a grizzly.

Yes, the animal tags were perfect, Cam decided. Jack Kenyon bore all the ideal traits of a terrier from the bushy beard and wiry body to the fearless barking disposition. Barking? What an understatement! Screaming was the better adjective, came her hasty correction, and screaming was one area where producer-director Kenyon excelled.

Cam watched Jack bounce further and further out of the backs of his boat shoes as his wildly gesturing hands enunciated every yelling statement: Didn't Devlin realize that he was holding up a film crew of over one hundred? That the animals alone cost two thousand dollars a day? That half a million big bucks had already been spent filming in this area during the last one hundred hours? That backdrops matching this area were being created by artists on a Hollywood sound stage right at this very moment?

Then, of course, there was Bridget. Cam had to admit the diminutive, wide-eyed Miss Lawson was proving herself to be equally bold and brave and fierce. She watched the silver screen's reigning sex goddess sway from side to side while shrieking about how valuable her time was; that any production delays would cause her to forfeit her next movie role; and as soon as she could find a phone, her lawyer was going to sue everybody!

And what about the growling villain of the piece? Up on her right elbow, head balanced in the palm of her hand, Cam's blue eyes focused a narrow attentive gaze on Thor Devlin. He was showing all the skilled fighting instincts of his Norse god namesake.

A smile slid over her lips as she listened to the deft way his rumbling voice hammered back with crisp, clean, to-the-point verbal counterpunches. Quite a contrast to Jack and Bridget's pompous bombastic display.

All of a sudden, Cam watched Thor do a complete reversal. He ceased arguing, his stance became military-straight, arms folded across his chest, eyes staring at some speck in the distance. The man had shut down. She studied the expression on his face and sighed. If his look could be translated Thor Devlin was totally disgusted and more than a little hostile.

"That's no way to handle this particular man," Cam mumbled. Lounging back across the boulder, eyes closed to the bright sun, she could imagine what was going through Thor's mind. "Probably thinks we're all cavemen. We certainly dress and act the part!"

Thor effortlessly tuned out the oral slings and arrows being thrown by producer and star. He wondered where he had misplaced not only his dignity but his normally friendly disposition as well.

Talk about turning a molehill into the Great Divide!

His lips tightened and thinned during his mental tongue-lashing. *Hell, this area of the ranch is good for nothing. If the federal government gave their permission to use Glacier Park, why in hell am I putting up such a damn fuss?*

He knew he was acting like a selfish, spoiled child who wouldn't let anyone else play with his toys. A rather disgusting image. A very tarnished image. An image that would be difficult to polish, especially with the three young boys who were riding with the wranglers.

Abruptly, Thor became aware that the movie company's cast and crew had steadily multiplied, courtesy of the helicopters. Now, more than his own people watched him act the fool. Morose eyes stared at this expanded, interested audience of nearly two dozen hulking actors with their bulging foreheads and dress resembling prehistoric man. Thor swallowed uncomfortably, silently judging himself to be the definitive Neanderthal.

There's no easy way out of this mess, came Thor's silent verdict. *The only way to save face is to play the tough, silent bastard and walk away. Just maybe they'll run scared and leave. Then she'll be gone.*

She!

His eyes widened. Damn, he was still thinking about her! Cam Stirling. How was it possible she had etched herself so quickly and deeply into his subconscious? Hell, until thirty minutes ago he never knew she existed and now—dammit, now *he* felt afraid and weak.

Afraid and weak. Thor gave an inward snicker at even acknowledging two such unmanly emotions. After all, how could there be anything about this woman to fear? *Perhaps if I take her apart. I can shake this . . . this . . .* Thor swallowed hard. He didn't know what *this* was!

30

Shifting position slightly, he made Cam Stirling more than just a shapely reflection that shimmered in the corner of his eye. Her pose was relaxed, hand splayed amid rambunctious golden curls, supple body and shapely legs formed an S curve. It took Thor a long moment to realize that she wasn't comfortably ensconced on a padded chaise but sunning herself on a rock.

Much to his chagrin, the longer and more critical his dissection, Thor discovered that parts of Cam Stirling were equal and sometimes better than the whole. She reminded him of a chameleon, easily adapting herself to any situation or surrounding. Thor instinctively knew here was a woman who could be knee-deep in mud and three hours later look elegant at a party. She was one of a kind. A woman whose style couldn't be catalogued.

With that silent admission and recognition, Thor again experienced fear and weakness. Not a manly cold-sweat fear but a fear that snaked along his flesh leaving a pleasurable burn. And the weakness was not one that incapacitated his body but threatened his soul, threatened his very singular existence.

It was the culmination of those feelings more than anything else that made Thor raise his arm in a threatening gesture and in a fierce voice state, "This is private land and you are trespassing." He turned, gave a clipped order for his men to mount up, then spurred his buckskin stallion into a gallop toward the woods.

Jack mopped the sweat dripping off his face with his forearm. "I—I thought he was going to hit me," came his faltering squeak. "I honestly did." He turned to Bridget. "Did you see Devlin's eyes? They went from blue to ice."

"The man's insane," the actress stated. "Look at this, my damn hands are shaking. I need a cigarette." Bridget looked around, spotted the wardrobe matron, and beckoned to her. One hand greedily pulled the half-burned smoke from the woman's lips; her other hand yanked the cigarette pack from the matron's smock pocket. "I need these more than you, sweetie." Wisps of menthol punctuated Bridget's "What now?"

"How about copies of Dale Carnegie's *How to Win Friends and Influence People.*"

They turned and stared at Cam. Smiling, she rearranged herself Indian-style on the limestone boulder and straightened the chamois loincloth. "For heaven's sake, where did you two drop your winning personalities? Jack, I've heard you fire people with more charm than you dealt Mr. Devlin. And Bridget, you've smashed cameras over reporters' heads with more finesse than you used just now."

Jack opened his mouth to yell, then thought better of it. "Oh, hell, you're right." Stubby fingers scratched his chest through the damp navy T-shirt. "I shouldn't have been so heavy-handed."

"Heavy lipped," Cam corrected. "Although I'm not so sure your usual good-ole-boy approach would have worked either."

Jack's dark eyes widened. "Money!" He snapped his fingers. "I should have offered the guy some bucks."

Bridget sucked to life another cigarette. "You *were* throwing around the numbers," she agreed. "Perhaps our gruff Montana rancher was just waiting for the dollar sign to be tossed in his direction." Her eyes narrowed on Cam. "Now, why are you shaking your head?"

"Because Luthor Devlin is not the type to hold out for a few Ben Franklins."

"Hey, I don't expect to buy the guy cheap," Jack returned. "I'll go for a Grover Cleveland or even a James Madison if I have to." He pulled his baseball cap further down on his forehead. "Every man has his price."

32

Cam puzzled that statement and again shook her head. "No, not every man. Especially not *this* man."

Jack sighed. "All right," he grumbled, "what would you have done?"

"Tried the commonsense approach."

"I did that." He turned to Bridget. "Wasn't I doing that?" At her nod, he folded triumphant arms across his chest. "See."

"No, you *yelled* it," Cam responded. "People do not listen to yelling. And it was very apparent that Devlin tuned the both of you out."

"You're saying I should talk to him again and this time try it quiet and controlled?" At her silent affirmation, Jack exhaled forcefully. "Listen, honey, I was born screaming. Everyone knows I live to yell. Hell, I even speak three decibels louder than normal. So calm and gentle lets me out." His gaze fixed on his voluptuous star. "How about you trying your feminine charms on Devlin?"

Bridget pretended to consider his request while she brushed loose tobacco off her ample, sun-bronzed cleavage. "Let me get this straight. You're asking me to play the role of the sacrificial virgin?"

The producer's lips thinned. "Sweetie, the only virgins in the immediate area are the trees. I'm just asking you to—"

"I know what you're asking. No way."

"Meaning he can't do anything for your career?"

"Jack, I'm warning you to watch that ugly little tongue of yours," Bridget's voice was low and mean. "You've been riding me hard since we started this damn film—"

"That's because every movie you work on runs three times its projected budget! And as for hard! Lady, I can always cut off those meals you're having flown in from Perino's."

"Don't you dare!" The threat was rasped between even white teeth. "I may be playing the part of a savage, but I refuse to be treated like one off camera."

"I'll treat you any way I damn well please!"

Bridget hissed and raised her hand to strike his face.

Quickly, Cam stepped between the two ready-to-spar adults. She caught Bridget's wrist as her forearm knocked back Jack's flailing hand, then aimed a chastising glance at their hostile expressions. "My, my, aren't we a volatile twosome today."

Grunting in disgust, Jack settled on the rock Cam had just vacated and scraped the red moss with his shoes. It was a full five minutes before his breathing and blood pressure returned to normal. "Now I know why I always hire a Stirling to do the stunt work in my films," came his chagrined rejoinder. "You not only can throw a punch but stop them as well."

She gave a carefree shrug. "What can I say? I come from a family of born peacemakers."

Bridget sniffed and lit yet another cigarette. "Then why not extend your peacemaking talents to our recalcitrant rancher?"

"Well, what do you know, for once a star has a brilliant idea," Jack chided. "Take a chopper, Cam, and see what you can do. Don't be afraid to offer him money. Go as high as five grand." His expression was suddenly pensive. He jerked a thumb toward the group of hulking stunt men. "Take one of the boys with you just in case there's trouble. I—"

"There won't be any trouble, Jack." Her eyes glinted with anticipation. "I dare the devil every day, why not Luthor Devlin!"

Nate was the first to hear the rotor blades that lashed above the sound of a dozen trotting horses. "Looks like we're gonna find us a visitor when we get home," he caroled to Thor. "Any bets on who it'll be?"

Blue eyes squinted at the helicopter that hovered briefly before quickly advancing. "Never was much of a bettin' man, Nate."

"Well, I just hope it ain't that runt of a screechin' director. Him and that female movie star gave me one beejezus of a headache. 'Course we could get lucky and find it's the cat lady. Take any bets on that?" Nate's raucous cackle didn't wait for Thor's reply.

Fifteen minutes later all bets were answered. Seeing the pleased expression on Thor's face, Nate decided that twelve would definitely be a crowd. He directed the wranglers toward the stables, droning to the three teen-agers his usual speech on the care and feeding of their animals.

Thor edged his horse next to the corral gate for a closer inspection of Cam Stirling. She had exchanged her skimpy costume for a man's white T-shirt and well-worn, stonewashed jeans. Her hair was in the same sexy tumble, though this time the blond curls were trying to thwart a white terry headband.

She was smiling and seemed quite comfortable despite her position. An index finger pushed the brim of his black Stetson higher off his forehead. "How do you do that?"

"Do what?"

"Sit cross-legged on a narrow fence rail. You're balanced like a-an elf."

"Invite me in for a glass of ice cubes with anything and I just might tell you."

"Ice cubes?"

Cam nodded. "That's the one thing in very short supply at our camp." His crooked half grin became more tantalizing with each passing second. And she realized if he kept on staring at her with those beautiful pale

35

Paul Newman blue eyes, she was going to need a block of ice just to stabilize her body temperature! With great difficulty, she met his gaze.

Thor caught his breath. Her black pupils had widened into opaque pools of onyx. The effect was enormously pleasurable and slightly hypnotic. The longer he stared at her, the more he forgot about the things around him: the ranch, the livestock, the men, his own fears. Nothing made an impression. Nothing but Cam Stirling.

Her smile deepened for a brief moment, then began to fade. "Now, don't tell me you haven't got an ice cube to spare?"

"Climb aboard. I'll ride you to the main house for a drink that's loaded with ice."

She liked the look of his hand on her arm. His lean brown fingers were strong and callused and decidedly masculine against her skin. Despite the summer heat, Cam felt a shiver of pure feminine awareness slither down her spine. A minute later, with her arms wrapped around his waist, she luxuriated in the warmth of his sinewy body.

"That was a very skillful transition from fence rail to the back of my saddle," came Thor's admiring statement.

"I'll let you in on a little secret." Her chin rested comfortably on his broad shoulder, her mouth spoke close to his ear. "Your saddle skirt and rolled-up rain slicker are much more comfortable than that splintery rail."

Laughter rumbled deep in his chest. "I have a feeling sitting on a regular chair will be quite a novelty for you." His right leg pressed against the stallion's side, edging him left toward the rein that touched his neck. His spurs nudged the horse forward in an easy walking gait.

"Your property is beautiful. Very impressive both from the ground and the air."

Thor's voice echoed the happy expression on his face. "Thanks. We do have a rather unique piece of land. The boundaries spill along Glacier Park, the Flathead and down to the Hungry Horse Dam." He was finding enormous pleasure in having Cam this close. He stared down at her hands that had settled against the silver buckle of his belt and felt her soft full breasts pressing into his back. His tone grew husky. "We run nearly a thousand head of beef cattle here and breed some mighty fine horses."

"Like this one?" Cam patted the stallion's light yellowish-gray flank.

"No. I found Peg running wild in the mountains three years ago."

"Hardly a very masculine name," she chided.

He turned his head and grinned. "Pegasus. One of the younger boys who spent the summer here named him. But not after reading Greek mythology. He got the name from one of those adventure cartoon shows."

Cam laughed. "Ah, that's much better and quite the perfect moniker. The way his black mane and long tail spread at full gallop, he does appear to fly." She remembered something that he'd said and queried, "Tell me about these Fresh Air kids."

"There's about a half-dozen ranchers beside myself that take in city kids for six weeks during the summer," Thor explained. "The boys come from all walks of life. This year two were sent by the juvenile courts as part of their probation. We take them out of the push-button society, work them hard, give them a new respect for themselves and the land."

"How many boys?"

"This year ten: one on one for each wrangler."

"That's really wonderful. Most people write the

check, take the deduction, and turn away but you—why you're actually spending time and giving yourself to—" Suddenly, her breath literally caught in her throat.

"What's the matter?" Thor countered sharply. "You okay?"

"Sorry." For a brief second, she felt foolish. "It's your house. The aerial view doesn't do it justice. Sitting high up on the sloping ground, it's as if—as if Nature embraced it and hugged it to her breast."

Thor increased the pressure on the reins, effectively stopping the saddle horse. Turning his head, he stared at her thoughtfully before he spoke. "The original house was built in that spot just for the view. That was back in 1870, when my great-great-grandfather gave up gold mining in Grasshopper Creek for cattle ranching.

"He fell in love with this isolated triangle of land between the mountains. Bought all the land from horizon to horizon. Each generation has added rooms to the main house and the current modern conveniences. But the view from every window is the same." His voice was rife with emotion. "The horizon bends up on all sides into the mountain ranges."

Cam took in every aspect of the sprawling natural log structure. "You can see the craftsmanship, feel the warmth and the love. That wraparound screen porch makes me think of my own home."

"No fancy Hollywood digs?"

She thumped his curled hat brim and mimicked his lazy drawl. "Sorry, pardner, but I'm just a ranch girl." Cam effortlessly slid off the horse's rump and grinned up at Thor. "We live in the Santa Ynez Valley, just north of Santa Barbara through the Los Padres National Forest. You can see the Sierra Madres from our front porch. Our thousand acres supports a dozen horses, a hundred head of beef, one milk cow, fifty chickens, two roosters, five dogs, three barn cats, my parents, two grandmothers, three brothers, me, and—"

"—a partridge in a pear tree."

Her eyes leisurely skimmed his firm athletic body while he dismounted. "No, but we do have a llama who can usually be found eating our apple tree."

He was laughing as he held open the screen door. "I'm afraid I can't offer you a sight as exotic as a llama."

"But you have something better. Ice cubes."

Thor crooked his finger. "Follow me, the kitchen's right through here."

"Nice and cool." She took a deep breath. "And something smells delicious. Hmm, homemade biscuits." Licking her lips, Cam scanned the open, bubbling pots on the double-sized gas range. "Potatoes. Green beans." Wrinkling her nose, she added, "Broccoli. Oh my, look at the size of these trout!"

"Our cook, Bud, spent the morning fishing the mountain streams."

She surveyed the lemon-garnished marinating entrées with wistful eyes. "Well, you're going to feast tonight."

He turned from investigating the contents of the refrigerator. "There's iced tea, lemonade, cola, orange, apple, and tomato juice, and," Thor held up his choice, "beer. Take your pick."

"Orange juice with—"

"Plenty of ice," he supplied.

While Thor was busy preparing her drink, Cam nonchalantly wandered around the big country kitchen. The color scheme was dominated by shades of green, from the spring ferns on the wallpaper to the avocado tones of the modern appliances. Cabinets and countertops were in the butcher block pattern; underfoot were shiny, earth slate tiles. A massive oak plank table was centered in the breakfast nook, affording the diners a stunning view of rolling green acres and soaring blue shadowed mountains profiled in the bay window.

She inspected the herb garden growing in the greenhouse bubble that had been cut into the outside wall. "Your cook would get along famously with my grandmother Maggie. She's forever snipping parsley and sprouting bean seeds for salads." Cam smiled her thanks and accepted the tall, ice-filled glass. "Hmm, this certainly hits the spot."

"Enough ice for you?" Thor inquired lazily, settling himself into a padded dining chair. "Have a seat."

Cam shook her head yes and no. She was having a difficult time getting to the point of her visit but her host didn't seem to be in a rush to get rid of her. "So, tell me more about that great-great-grandfather of yours," she invited, lounging against the counter. "I believe you said he was a gold miner."

"Yup, drank and gambled and caroused his way through three fortunes. Grampa Luke moved from one wild mining camp to another before the love of a good woman tamed him." Thor watched Cam's smile broaden. "He was even part of the vigilante committee that hanged Henry Plummer in 1864."

"Henry Plummer?"

"Plummer was an outlaw leader who duped the settlers into making him sheriff. The good citizens of Bannack and Virginia City decided to rid themselves of the outlaws and became vigilantes. Their symbols were the numbers three, seven, seventy-seven." At her raised eyebrow, Thor explained, albeit a bit sheepishly. "Those numbers represented the dimensions of a grave: three feet wide, seven feet long, and seventy-seven inches deep."

Her eyes locked with Thor's. "Three, seven, and seventy-seven. Hmm, that's a bit too big for Jack Kenyon's body but much too small for his ego." She smiled as she watched his mustachioed upper lip twitch. "He and Bridget were rather full of themselves and supercilious."

Thor sluiced the condensation off the amber beer bottle. "That also sounds like an excellent description of me." He took a hefty swig of lager while waiting for her reply. When none was forthcoming, his mouth twisted in a crooked smile. "Discretion the better part of valor?"

Cam held out her empty glass. "I'd never dream of contradicting such a gracious host."

After pouring her another eight ounces of orange juice, Thor calmly folded his hands across his chest. "So, now we come to the real purpose of your visit. Did Kenyon send you to exercise your sex appeal and make me change my mind?"

"If I were going to use sex, I'd have left my costume on." Cam pulled out a chair and sat down at the table. She was supremely conscious of a pair of ice-blue eyes that charted her every move. "Actually, Jack instructed me to offer you money, but I told him you weren't the type of man that could be bought—at least with cash."

"And what currency would you use?"

"Logic and reason."

His hands made an expansive gesture. "So, go ahead, reason with me."

The closed expression on Thor's face held her back. Cam mentally dithered over how best to proceed. Should she try being cool, aloof, and businesslike? Or would that prove more irritating? She wanted to touch him, to place her hand on his arm, just a companionable gesture. But would he take it the wrong way and think she was being sexual just to get him to change his mind?

And yet, she couldn't seem to shake the need to touch Thor. So Cam did the next best thing. She reached across the table for his hat. Her fingertips

41

stroked the brim, moving on to trace the silver conchos that encircled the squared crown. When she finally spoke, she heard herself stuttering and stammering like a child anxious to forestall an adult's wrath.

"Well, um, let me just add that it was truly by accident that we strayed off government land. The park rangers are dealing with a record number of tourists, campers, and hikers, so after two days of dos and don'ts, they left us on our own. We scouted the area, searching for the right locations, and found a unique natural foursome that fit the script."

Cam hesitated a moment as an odd thought invaded her mind. She nervously wet her lips. "I'm almost afraid to ask this. Besides the escarpment, are the cliff and waterfall plus those double-humped mountains yours too?"

Thor nodded.

Her fingers drummed against the polished oak table-top. "Well, Mr. Devlin, it seems all of your land was scheduled to be the silent star of this movie. Quite frankly, I had a great deal to do with that selection and it's going to be a major hardship for me to go somewhere else."

"I don't understand."

"I've spent the last ten days getting to know the land, your land. There's a lot of planning in stunt work. Mentally and drawing-board type and . . ." Cam frowned. "Well, I'd have to start all over again. That's if I'm lucky enough to find what I need inside Glacier Park."

When Thor failed to reply, she continued, her voice soft. "We don't intend to destroy any part of your property, Thor. Ramon may eat a few trees here and there but we'd be glad to replant." His sudden smile made her visibly relax. "Would it really be such an inconvenience if we stayed and finished this movie?"

Thor took his time before answering. His eyes had

caught and held the sensual movements of her mouth. Now his brain was hard at work trying to restore equilibrium to the rest of his body. While his outward appearance was cool, almost aloof, inside Thor found himself captivated in mind and body.

Silly. Adolescent. Sophomoric. Those were the perfect adjectives to describe him. Words that he'd long outgrown. But Thor felt positively invigorated about having all those feelings and found himself growing increasingly possessive about the woman who so easily created them—possessive enough to want her to stay.

His thumb and forefinger smoothed the thick brown hairs on his mustache. "How much money is Kenyon willing to offer?"

Cam eyed him curiously. "Up to five thousand."

"A nice round figure," he grinned and rubbed his hands together. "That's a hefty donation for your boss to make to the local children's shelter and so very tax deductible."

Her laugh was one of pure delight. "You are a very clever man, Luthor Devlin. Jack will like the deduction part, it'll ease the pain when he writes that check." She was thoughtful a moment. "I hope you won't take offense at my next request but would you mind putting your permission in writing?"

"Not at all. Let's adjourn to my study and make this all nice and official."

She lagged behind Thor, her interest shifting for a time from the man to his environment. Cam had always thought you could tell a lot about a person from their home and despite the fact that this house was a collection of rooms added from one generation to another, the imprint of the latest Devlin was unmistakable.

Stepping through the kitchen's saloon doors into the great room living area, Cam was made even more aware of Montana's natural beauty by the wall of windows.

Here, before her eyes, a real-life pastoral scene was in constant motion: mares and foals cavorting in the home paddock against a backdrop dominated by the rugged, wild beauty of the mountains.

The room's furnishings were comfortable, casual, and decidedly masculine. Two sofas, the leather covering worn to a shiny patina, formed an L in front of a hand-cut stone fireplace, its limestone mantel displaying framed photos, silver mugs, and some odd heirloom bric-a-brac. The sense of family was strong and she liked that. Pausing to study the pictures, Cam inquired, "Is your vigilante grandfather one of these?"

"No, but his rifle is the top one on the gun rack, the one with the canteen hanging on it."

"At least you haven't given the local taxidermist any business," she commented. "I've worked with such a diverse group of animals that seeing anything that was killed for sport stuffed and mounted for decoration makes me angry and ill."

"When I shoot at all it's with a camera. This," Thor's hand dropped to his gun holster, "is used to scare. Everyone on the ranch, including the boys, have respect for wildlife and are taught when and how to handle firearms." He pushed open a carved door and gestured toward an overstuffed chair. "Have a seat while I type."

Cam looked around the comfortable room that boasted a wall of black metal file cabinets, drafting board, bookcases, and a massive desk. "I see this room lacks a window."

"Too distracting." He grinned, rolling paper into the platen of a ten-year-old manual typewriter. "I compensated with a print of Charlie Russell's *When the Land Belonged to God.*"

"That cowboy artist can certainly paint," she agreed. "I'm planning on stopping at the Historical Society Museum in Helena before I leave. I want to see his other paintings, the bronzes, and read a few of those whimsical letters he wrote to Will Rogers."

"Your time will be well spent. You might even try to visit Russell's original studio in Great Falls." Thor pulled the finished document from the typewriter, reread what he'd written, corrected a typo with a pen, then scrawled his name. "There you go. Now you can do me one little favor."

Cam folded the agreement and tucked it in her back pocket. "What's that?"

"Rearrange our little conversation about the donation any which way that will make Kenyon feel the hero." At her inquiring glance, he gave a sheepish smile, then explained. "This just gives me a graceful way out of a situation that escalated from the sublime to the ridiculous to the outrageous."

This time, Cam didn't hesitate, her hand closed against his wrist. "You were caught off-guard," she readily protested. "Out tracking rustlers and finding yourself involved in . . . in prehistoric hysterics."

Thor's left hand settled on top of hers. "I appreciate your defense but—"

"Say, maybe we can do you a favor," she interrupted, seeing how uncomfortable he was. "How about if we keep an eye out for those cattle thieves. Our helicopter camera crew has certain advantages."

He considered her offer for a second. "Frankly, I'd welcome the help. Six of our animals have been slaughtered already. At this rate, the rustlers will be netting a dozen or more a month."

"From you alone?" she inquired.

"No. There are thirty of us. So far we're out nearly three million in livestock and equipment."

Cam whistled. "Ouch! Rustling in California is big business too."

"Rustling's always been big and despite using freeze

brands and photos and varying ranch routine, we are still getting hit."

"I'll alert our helicopter crews and maybe we can give you all a helping hand." From the living room a cuckoo clock chirruped the time, making Cam frown. "I'd better get going."

Thor boldly recaptured her hand. "I was hoping you'd stay for dinner. If the host isn't tempting enough, maybe the trout and an endless supply of ice cubes will do."

She noted the gleam in his eyes and matched it with one of her own. "That's a very tempting offer, but Jack's scheduled some night shooting, and now that the location problem's settled it won't do to hold up production." Cam took a chance and asked, "Can I get a rain check?"

"Anytime." Reluctantly he led her out the front door. "Besides, you still owe me the secret of your fence sitting."

"So I do." Her voice lowered in a conspiratorial whisper. "Maybe you'd like to learn an even bigger secret."

"What's that?"

Cam turned and began to walk backward. "Come to the escarpment tomorrow at sunrise and—"

"And what?" He watched her laugh and shake her head. "Come on, Cam!" Thor moved to grab her arm but found he missed her by the proverbial mile. "Cam!" Her vivacious, teasing personality made him feel even more alive and stimulated. "And what?"

She stopped running and turned to look at him. With his hands on his hips, Thor stood tall and invincible. The western sun cast a halolike glow around his sculpted head, making his curly hair appear to be on fire.

Cam squinted Thor's face into focus and came to the

unwavering decision that this was the man she had to see first thing tomorrow morning. "And bring breakfast, Mr. Devlin!" She yelled. "A big breakfast!" Then she raced for the helicopter she had parked in the empty home pasture.

CHAPTER THREE

A woman. A mountain. A sunrise. For Thor the day pulsed with promise.

Reining Pegasus on a ridge that overlooked the bustling film crew, Thor also found he had an advantageous position to view the activity on the escarpment. The female silhouette was joined by that of a big cat's, their sleek forms cavorting with playful abandon.

Thor sat watching and wondering, wanting and wavering. The tension that had alternately crippled and pleasured his body for most of the night was again manifesting itself. The source of that tension? Thor resignedly had to admit it was Cam Stirling.

She had dominated his thoughts. He had willed and waited for her initial impact to fade. But the illuminated clock on his night table mocked his stalwart intentions. Fade? Hell, the more determined he was to forget Cam Stirling the more her invisible presence seemed to intrude on his thoughts.

A self-derisive smile twisted Thor's lips as he gave himself a disciplining shake. What in hell had gotten into him? Yesterday he acted the Neanderthal, during the night he'd become a casebook randy schoolboy with a stupid crush.

"And I always thought of myself as a very happy, content, well-adjusted, independent man." Thor spoke out loud, his voice firm and controlled. He was chagrined to note that his brain and body were not equally harnessed.

"This is insane and I am a fool." Leaning forward in the saddle, his exhaled breath caused Pegasus' ears to twitch. "We have cattle to check, rustlers to track, chores to complete, and here we sit at five in the morning, breakfast in hand, waiting for a woman to come down from a mountain!"

Thor refocused on the escarpment, his mind contemplating that distant scene, when suddenly Cam and the cat began to move. Slowly at first, then their speed increased until Thor doubted his eyes.

As they were yesterday, woman and feline duplicated each other's supple, animal grace. Neither seemed to notice that they were on a rugged, flat-topped plateau over two thousand vertical feet in height. Or that the jagged limestone offered the dangerous gift of loose mantlerock and fault scarps.

But Thor noticed.

His body jumped and shrank at the same time. He tried to shout but found his vocal cords paralyzed. Only his eyes were mobile. And it was a pair of very anxious eyes that tracked Cam's leap from pinnacle to pinnacle until her haloed silhouette finally came to rest against the crimson sky.

An odd, strangled, choking sound assailed Thor's ears. He was shocked to discover the noise came from his own lungs as they greedily gulped in the crisp morning air. Wiping cold, sweaty hands against his jeans, Thor stared in wonder at the mesa while waiting for the numbness to dissipate from his body.

Whirling helicopter blades exploded the silence. Twisting in his saddle, Thor shifted his attention to the rising chopper and watched it level with the top of the butte. He could hear but not understand the bullhorned instructions.

Then a second and much larger copter gyred into the sky. This one had a man in a catbird seat holding a camera. Thor observed its maneuvers with confused interest before vigilantly returning to sight Cam.

It took him a few seconds to find her. She and the cat had returned to their original positions. Thor heard additional amplified directives as the camera-manned copter was piloted in a stabilized hover.

Teeth clamped down against his lower lip, Thor's heart seemed to beat brutally in his throat and his breathing became virtually nonexistent as Cam again conquered the mountain. The scene was continually replayed with only the helicopter's changing positions.

Two hours later, after it all ended, Thor had to work hard to relax the muscles in his body. The initial shock and fear he experienced over Cam had evolved into awe and fascination, and the need to know everything about her.

Enthusiastic applause greeted her as she dropped to the ground from the helicopter's rope ladder. Even a two-fingered whistle of approval reverberated from producer/director Jack Kenyon. But all the while Cam was waving her thanks, her eyes kept searching the crowd for one special face.

She had been sweating out the possibility that he wouldn't show up. Then she saw him. He was standing about three hundred feet away, sheltered by a grove of aspen, the buckskin stallion at his side. The smile that curved her lips was formed by pure delight rather than gratefulness for the fleece bathrobe and wool leg warmers the wardrobe matron was wrapping around her.

After checking out with the assistant director, Cam journeyed to where Thor was waiting. Her pace paralleled her thoughts: slow and cautious. Her subconscious quickly taunted that last night, her thoughts were anything but slow and cautious!

She used the wide collar on the peach robe to hide the little girl blush that suffused her cheeks. Thor had monopolized her thoughts and starred in her dreams. And Cam's dreams hadn't been little girlish either. Womanly, yes. Passionate, very. Lusty, most assuredly!

Cam tried to make sense of her reactions but couldn't. *Chemistry.* The word popped into her mind. Her mother and maternal grandmother called it that intangible something that makes your blood boil and common sense drown in a sea of desire. Their giggling vividly echoed in Cam's ears before bubbling between her own lips.

Resolutely, she cleared her throat and groped for equilibrium. This—this chemistry schmaltz only worked on TV or in movies or in novels. Oh, all right, Cam reminded herself, maybe it had happened to both her mother and grandmother but—but, well, that was a different time, a different moral climate.

Today, romance resembled a business. There were new courtship rules like splitting checks and sex on the third date. If you said no men thought you were weird or a prude. But in Cam's mind casual sex was like a diet of junk food—instantly gratifying but hardly substantial or permanently satisfying.

She was very realistic about love and had literally closed down any business with romance. Being single was fine; she didn't need a man to make her a complete woman. Then, too, there was her career. A stunt woman needed a level head. No emotional roller coasters allowed.

Lifting her gaze from the ground, Cam discovered Thor's rugged physique and strong male presence becoming more formidable, more irresistible with her every step. And she found herself overcome with a burning desire to know what his lips felt like against hers. So much for realism and the flat light of day disputing the mysterious laws of romantic chemistry!

Fingers that were anxiously filtering through her hair reformed into a flirty wave. Talk about a dichotomy— while her hand was playing the coquette, her stomach had become a haven for butterflies. From that candid and rather silly appraisal of her feelings, Cam found her giggles returning.

That giddy release effectively cleared her head. The same calmness and serenity that always preceded her stunt work now mastered her actions and censored her thoughts. As she approached Thor, Cam's smile was wide and friendly, her mind and heart open. "Good morning."

When he failed to respond, Cam was perplexed. "Isn't the sunrise glorious?" Nothing verbal but the muscle in Thor's cheek flexed.

From the robe's pocket, she produced a sugar cube purloined from the coffee wagon and offered it to Pegasus, who whinnied his thanks. "At last a greeting!" But Thor remained an enigma.

Cam peered into his face and wondered what happened. Yesterday they had shared warm smiles and laughter, this morning more than the air was crisp. Her index finger snapped against the brim of his black Ştetson. "Don't tell me you're the type who doesn't speak before noon."

"I guess I'm still in a state of shock." He hadn't meant to say that.

Her eyes widened inquiringly. "Something happen at the ranch? Was it one of the boys?"

Inhaling deeply, Thor strove to remain impassive but the words and emotions he'd kept in check tumbled out on their own volition. "No . . . here. You. Up there.

Running. Loose rocks. Danger." He stopped, realizing he wasn't making much sense.

Cam was, at once, both surprised and moved by Thor's concern. Her hand settled on his arm. Her touch was tender, her voice reassuring. "There wasn't any real danger but if you thought that, then I did my job very well." Her clear blue eyes smiled into his troubled ones. "I have to make people believe there's peril—"

"You're telling me there wasn't?"

"I never leave anything to chance," she returned matter-of-factly. "I've spent the last week making sure the top of the escarpment was smooth, solid, and hazard-proof. And there's a furry colony of orange-bellied marmots that supervised my every move!"

Noting a more relaxed attitude in Thor, Cam continued. "Actually, my biggest problem was with the cat. Pumpkin hates to ride in a helicopter and I don't think he's all that fond of heights. A classic acrophobic."

She watched him lower his head and peer up at her as if looking over invisible bifocals. The corners of his blue eyes crinkled and his lips curved in a happier configuration. "You have quite a nuts-and-bolts attitude."

"This is ordinary for me," Cam responded easily. "Just as . . . hmm . . . riding a horse is for you."

"Yeah, but there's no danger—"

"Tell that to someone who's been *thrown* off a horse! Everything is relative."

Thor discovered he had an overwhelming need to know that she was really safe. "I'm not sure I buy that argument," he persisted. "You were moving pretty fast and one slip—"

"I was running a steady gait. In fact, Jack had to mount a wide-angle lens on the camera to give a greater impact of speed." At his puzzled expression, she explained. "The wider the lens, the faster the action because it's the sides of the picture that really create the feeling of speed.

"Thor, I work in a celluloid fantasy where illusions are greater than reality." She squeezed his arm, liking a little too much the warmth and strength of his hair-roughened flesh. "Just remember, nothing is what it appears to be."

His left hand moved to clasp and secure her wrist, her pulse an intoxicating rhythm against his fingers. Thor's deep, husky timbre inquired, "And what about you, Cam Stirling? Are you what you appear to be? Are you real or just another Hollywood illusion?"

Eyes locking into his, her manner was femininely compelling. "Oh, I'm very real, Luthor Devlin, and—" Cam's lashes made a provocative flutter but when she spoke, her voice lilted with laughter "—very hungry! I hope those saddlebags are filled with breakfast."

A long, masculine finger gently silhouetted the short, straight line of her nose. "Overflowing," came Thor's easy rejoinder. Her instant smile warmed him, as did her presence. And all those contented, relaxed feelings of well-being that he experienced yesterday with Cam returned.

She watched Thor turn to unpack their breakfast. Hearing his cheery whistle, Cam's grin broadened. Her gaze fastened on his strong, sunburned hands as they loosened the buckles on the saddlebags and the sinewy flexing of his back muscles beneath the denim shirt.

Cam stared at Thor's nape, noticing his hair needed a trim, but liking the way the thick brown waves coiled along his shirt collar. Imagining those rich, virile curls twined around her fingers made her feel quite intoxicated and decidedly wonderful.

Maybe it was her masculine companion, her intimate musings, the blush searing her breasts and moving upward to her face—or all those things put together that caused Cam to take a giant mental step backward.

Good grief! She blinked rapidly. *Where are these thoughts, these reactions, and these daydreams coming from? I've worked with the major macho hunks of television and motion pictures and remained unflappable.* "Why him?"

Thor turned his head. "What was that?"

Cam swallowed hard. Had she actually *said* something? "Ah—ah—breakfast!" came her stuttered excuse. "Where is all this overflowing food you promised?"

"Right here." He tossed a large Thermos at her.

"This is it?" She made a face. "We action technicians do not live by—" shaking the container, she guessed, "coffee alone."

"Hot chocolate," he countered. "And I'm anxious to see just how well balanced you action technicians are."

With that cryptic remark, Cam found herself perilously juggling three Thermos bottles and battling for control. "I once doubled as a circus clown for a television movie of the week."

"Why am I not surprised?"

While her eyes followed the aerial high jinks of the tumbling bottles, her ears listed to Thor's further preparations. "Say, I hope there's something more substantial than chocolate in these varied containers."

"There certainly is and it's just about ready." Thor plucked two Thermoses from the air and watched as she caught the other one. "A veritable feast." Hat in hand, he made a flourishing gesture.

"I am impressed by your early morning elegance, Mr. Devlin. A red and white checked tablecloth, bright blue plates and cups, shiny silverware, and—my goodness," her left eyebrow rose, "white linen napkins."

"Careful, you're making me blush."

Her gaze was direct. "I think that's rather nice in a man." Thor's sheepish expression caused her to change the subject. "And what, pray tell, is the *pièce de résistance* of this repast?"

"Pull up, hmm, some earth and I'll show you." He marveled at the way she crossed her ankles and, with a polished ballet move, settled on the grass, the thick bathrobe serving as a cushion. "If I try that, I'll fall over." Thor gave a self-depreciating grin as he lowered himself next to Cam.

"This is a lovely luxury for me," she confided. "Breakfast is usually coffee in a Styrofoam cup, a couple of doughnuts, and, if I'm lucky, cold scrambled eggs."

Thor made a face. "Hardly the nutritious way to start the day, Miss Stirling." He poured steaming hot chocolate into her mug, adding a dozen tiny marshmallows, then reached for a wide-mouthed Thermos. "Here we have a fresh fruit compote. I'll bet Montana strawberries are bigger than California's."

"I'll concede that point," she returned, "but don't tell me these are Montana peaches, bananas, pears, and grapes."

His responding laugh was rich and genuine and it sent a delicious wave of sweet sensations coursing through her body. "Next on the list," Thor continued, "is something that is homegrown or, more correctly, homemade. Oversized flaky biscuits stuffed with ham and cheese plus link sausages and hard-boiled eggs that are still warm."

Cam discovered she had to concentrate very hard to understand Thor's words over the sensual movements of his lips. For her, the chemistry between them was crackling, filling the air with heady tension, lovely anticipation, and the delicious confusion of wondering where this encounter would lead.

He placed one of everything on her plate, then teased, "I did promise you overflowing."

"I do like a man who keeps his promises." Her tone was sweet and carefree but, Cam realized, uncharacteristically bold.

Glancing up from spooning the compote on his own plate, Thor was about to deliver a glib retort but found it dissolving on his tongue. She filled his eyes. His senses felt charged with a new intensity, a new vibrancy.

To Thor, Cam appeared vulnerable yet enormously sexy even though she was completely swathed in a robe and wool leg warmers. When a gentle breeze ruffled her tousled bangs, he experienced an astounding emotion—jealousy.

What was Thor jealous of? The wind! He didn't like the air so brazenly caressing her face. He wanted to be the one to brush back her hair. He needed to feel the softness of her skin against his fingers. And he was experiencing an irrepressible desire to kiss her full, ripe lips.

Cam held his gaze a long moment, then looked away. "You're—you're losing your strawberry." Quickly, she rescued the falling fruit but halfway to her mouth, her hand was captured by his.

"That does belong to me."

"Possession is . . ."

"Maybe the perfect solution would be to share it."

His voice was low, husky, and its effect on Cam decidedly hypnotic. She knew it was seven o'clock on a bright morning, the mountain air anything but torrid, yet she had the strangest feeling of being seduced. And she was liking it very much!

Leaning forward, Thor guided the strawberry into her mouth, watching Cam's even white teeth sink into the soft, succulent ruby-red pulp. The callused roughness of his fingers belied the tenderness of his touch. His undeniable maleness provoked a purely feminine response.

Her breathing came faster and her breasts seemed to swell. She became intensely aware of every square inch of her body, a body that yearned for a more intimate connection. Moving ever closer, Thor lowered his head and let his lips become a delicate napkin that blotted the sweet juice from her mouth.

The strawberry tumbled into oblivion. Cam's hand caressed his strong jawline, the soft skin on her palm finding pleasure in the masculine stubble. And when his butterfly kiss deepened with just a hint of increasing insistence, she emitted a soft, satisfied sigh.

This seems so right, so natural, so normal. Thor's subconscious issued that profound announcement as his tongue made a delicate foray into the honeyed recesses of her mouth. His fingers filtered through her platinum curls, luxuriating in the silken strands.

Again and again, his mouth claimed hers. Kisses soft. Kisses deep. Kisses tender. Kisses hungry. His body was hungry too. Craving to press against hers, hurting to know each womanly curve.

Thor knew he should slow down. But he didn't. He knew he should stop. But he couldn't. There was an urgency deep inside that kept driving him. Pushing him. Demanding that he make an indelible imprint *now.* An imprint that would brand Cam Stirling his forever.

It was Pegasus who brought them back to reality with a shower of gravel and pine needles, when a previously silent helicopter walloped into action. Scrambling to his feet, Thor quickly grabbed for the horse's reins, trying to calm the startled stallion before his hooves could do further trampling.

"No harm done," Cam announced, righting two fallen Thermos bottles and brushing debris off the tablecloth. She was desperately trying to understand how one strawberry, a simple fruit for heaven's sake, could turn into such a heady catalyst.

Eve probably had the same thought after the apple incident, came her silent chide. *But Eve lost paradise, while I—I tasted it.* Cam brushed a thick strand of hair from her face and wished this was a scene from a movie.

It was so much easier to work from a script. Every thought, every action, every line was written out and expertly directed. Real life was not so black and white. A person could make a mistake. One careless expression, one misspoken word, one odd action—and paradise could, indeed, be forfeited.

Her eyes focused on Thor, watching his gentle ministerings to his horse. Cam wondered what type of woman this man wanted and searched for a clue. Perhaps a flirtatious coquette? An aggressive seductress? A naive temptress?

Cam could be all of those. But what was she really? Sometimes shy. Sometimes bold. Sometimes the flirt. Sometimes the innocent. And while her stunt skills were graceful and precise, her previous dealings with men on a one-to-one, personal basis had been decidedly inept and incompetent.

Her fingers came up to massage her forehead. The more she thought, the more confused she became. So Cam decided to stop thinking, stop analyzing, stop hypothesizing—and just be herself.

No false fronts. No counterfeit emotions. No pretending to embrace someone else's ideals. Hadn't she, just three weeks ago, started her twenty-ninth year with a new take-me-as-I-am attitude?

Deciding things were moving too fast, Cam let intelligence triumph over her libido. So, when Thor returned to her side, she extended his plate with a pleasant, "Your breakfast is getting cold."

A smile slid across his face. "I doubt I'd notice." His

hand deliberately missed the dish, curving instead against the side of her neck. "You blush beautifully."

"And you move very fast."

His fingers toyed with the bear-claw necklace tied at her throat. "Usually I'm slow and plodding."

Now it was Cam's turn to smile. "Couldn't prove it by me."

Thor removed his hand and averted his eyes. "Confession time. I . . . well, hell, I figured I'd better work as fast as the Hollywood crowd."

Her eyebrow arched. "Never take *you* for reading those sleazy supermarket tabloids." Cam's index finger lifted his chin, her eyes bright. "Besides, did you forget that I'm not of the Hollywood crowd?"

"You run with them."

"Work for them," she corrected. Then she added, "And since when are civil engineers plodding? Slow, maybe; careful, definitely; cautious, always." Her finger tapped his nose. "The cautious seldom err."

Thor drew back his head, then lunged forward, snapping at her finger like a turtle. "I'm not erring now. Not with you." He kissed her finger. "Say, how did you know I'm a civil engineer?"

"Saw the diploma on the wall in your den. Tell me—"

Cam was interrupted as the main and tail rotors on the nearby second helicopter whirled into action, triggering a snorting Pegasus into an explosion of mule kicks.

An obviously annoyed Thor went again to quell the fears of his buckskin stallion. "What the devil are they doing now?" He yelled above the din.

She studied the chopper's maneuvers, waiting until both man and horse quieted down. "They're bringing Bridget up to the escarpment to do some cowboy close-ups."

"Cowboy close-ups?" He inquired, settling back on the cloth.

"That's a head-and-shoulder camera shot that will be cut in with my stunt work."

"Illusions again."

"Probably more than you realize," Cam confided. "Forty percent of this picture will be special effects and optical illusions. Jack grumbled all morning that the mountains appeared too gentle in the daily rushes. So, he commissioned another painting on glass that, when edited in, will make the escarpment blatantly forbidding."

Thor scratched his jaw. "You are going to have to translate. What are daily rushes?"

"It's the first film print of a scene that the director inspects to make sure he's getting what he wants."

"And glass paintings?"

Cam swallowed a mouthful of hot chocolate. "They're used all the time in movies to give," she smiled, "your favorite word again, the illusion of height. In, mmm, *Star Wars,* do you remember when Luke was walking on a rail, high above the cavernous control center?" Thor nodded. "Well, that was a painting on glass and the actor was, oh, no more than a dozen or so inches off the ground. The same technique was used in the Indiana Jones movies, most sci-fi ones, and those westerns that pop up now and again."

"I just never realized." He shook his head.

"Most people don't," she returned with a smile. "Some of the special effects take months of tedious work, often using miniatures of the actors and scenes that have to be changed and reshot every second.

"My two hours of running this morning will show up as a few seconds on film. And that's an excellent ratio. I just came from six weeks at the Indian Dunes in the Mexican desert. Forty-one of those days were spent set-

61

ting up an explosion stunt that will disappear in two blinks of an eye when you see it in the movie theater."

"What did you say was the name of this extravaganza?"

"Well, today, it's *Empress of Armageddon*," Cam's tone was highly exaggerated. "When we started the movie, it was *Warrior Goddess*."

"A sword and sorcery epic?" Thor queried.

"Only Jack knows for sure," she laughed. "He rewrites every day, shoots scenes out of order, and keeps increasing the number of special effects. From what I'm able to put together, the story takes place a millennium after a nuclear holocaust. Man and animals have progressed to the prehistoric stage with the exception of the empress—"

"Bridget Lawson."

"Right. Bridget is perfection incarnate in both the beauty and brains department. She is the only one who knows how to use postnuclear sorcery against an evil horde of men and monsters to free other perfect survivors."

Thor's confused expression and his vague "uh huh" made Cam add, "Trust me, it'll be dynamite on the silver screen. Jack has yet to lose a single penny on any of his productions. People see them over and over just to ooh and ahh over the dazzling special effects and, if I do say so myself, some incredible stunts."

Thor had difficulty swallowing a sausage past the lump that suddenly thickened his throat. He just kept staring at Cam. Earlier she had been able to quell his fears about her high-altitude run. Now, as he listened to her recitations of more dramatic and more dangerous stunts, fear again became his partner. Not only was he afraid for Cam's safety and well-being but Thor found himself under a siege of anxiety and panic. What if there was an accident? She admitted the stunts were incredible. What if she was hurt? She was working with explosives. What if Cam was killed? He couldn't stand to lose her—not when she had just been found.

It took Thor a few moments to bring his erratic breathing under control. He discovered, however, it was impossible to expel the menacing specters that invaded his mind.

To his eyes, everything about her appeared fragile. Her pastel robe and platinum hair, her softly rounded face and patrician features, her melodic voice and delicate mannerisms. Fragile. Vulnerable. In need of protection. *His* protection. And Thor was determined to provide that protection. When he opened his mouth to administer his viewpoint, Thor was surprised to hear another man's voice emerge.

"*Camilla,* ah, sorry to interrupt, but it's back to work you go." Darrell Booth clicked his tongue against the roof of his mouth. "Don't make such a face, darling." His keen gray eyes scrutinized her face. "You do need touching up. Okay, let's dump the robe." He began tugging apart the knotted peach sash.

When Cam saw Thor drop his plate, anger tainting his expression, she hurriedly made introductions. "Darrell is the supervising makeup man on this movie."

"Makeup ar-teest," Darrell corrected, one perfectly manicured hand combing through his blond crewcut. "I deserve an Oscar nomination." His words were directed toward Thor. "Do you know what it takes to turn two dozen men into Neanderthals? Well, I'll tell you what it takes. Genius. Three and a half hours of genius per Neanderthal!" Inhaling deeply, Darrell surveyed Thor. "Nice to meet you. Love the trim on your mustache."

The makeup man shifted his attention to Cam. "Your tan is fading. You won't match Bridget. Get more sun." Darrell's sigh was exaggerated. "I cannot handle extra stress, Camilla. Where's my number three?" He began rummaging amid an assortment of tubes, brushes, and sponges in the giant metal chest he was carrying.

"I didn't have anything scheduled until this afternoon."

"Kenyon's reshooting the jousting scene with the flying dinosaur from a different angle." He squirted base on his fingers and began slapping it on her shoulders and back.

Cam wrinkled her nose at Thor. "Sorry about this. I'm afraid illusionary pterodactyls replace my leisurely breakfast."

"Leisure? On a Jack Kenyon set?" Darrell snorted. He looked at Thor from between Cam's legs, his voice low and confiding. "Frankly, I think I'm putting bulging foreheads, scars, curved limbs, and extra hair on the wrong man. When Kenyon stands fully erect . . ."

"Darrell!" She tried unsuccessfully to control her laughter.

His tall, wiry body contorted around hers. "I am serious, darling. I know Kenyon's pictures make big bucks and garner awards but I swear the man has the IQ of lint when it comes to dealing with people. This is my first and last with him, award or no. I don't know how you've done—what? Three? Four?"

"Six."

"Six!" Standing up, Darrell winked at an impassive Thor. "Where is the halo polish?" His hands worked quickly, slapping body makeup on her breasts. "I don't know how you put up with—oops! What's this? A strawberry!" One blond brow arched. "Feeding our cleavage, are we, Camilla?"

She flicked the berry from its taunting dangled pose. "Just sloppy eating habits, Mr. Booth."

Darrell's smirking "indeed" encompassed both Cam and Thor. Her staid expression spoke volumes, causing Darrell to get back to business. He pulled a small notepad from the pocket of his one-piece, short pink jump-suit. "Ah, let's see, only thing left for you is the spray sweat."

"A wonderful mixture of oil and bug spray," Cam explained to Thor. "Not that I won't add a little natural sweat of my own."

"Not too much, darling," Darrell countered, giving her cleavage an extra squirt. "Water cannot highlight your wonderful muscles the way the oil does. And that's what Kenyon is after. He's showing off the magnificent beauty of the female form." He clapped his hands together. "Okay, sweetie, let's move. I'll take your robe. Walk neat. Don't kick up any dust."

"But—but . . ."

"No time." His index finger pushed into the base of her spine. "Let's go—go—go!"

Cam only had time to wave a hasty good-bye to Thor as Darrell cowed her back to the movie set.

On the outside, Thor appeared carved from stone. The inner man, however, was a myriad of contorted emotions. Logic and reason were pushed aside by an image that jabbed away at his masculine ego.

What was the image? Hands. Not Thor's clean, cal-lused hands. But Darrell Booth's slim, elegant, mani-cured hands. And where were his hands? On Cam Stir-ling. Her thighs. Her back. Her shoulders. Her neck. And between her breasts. Stroking her skin. Touching more than her flesh.

"His damn hands were all over her!" Thor bellowed. His balled fist slashed amid the remnants of the picnic breakfast, scattering dishes, cups, Thermos, and food in a thousand directions. "Ah, hell." His sudden anger left him exhausted.

He sat for a long while, trying not to think about Cam but failed. She had, in a very short time, made more than an impression, and maybe that was why his emotions were so on edge.

Exercise, he thought as he stood up. That's what he needed. Good, hard, head-clearing physical exercise.

Surveying the mess at his feet, Thor sighed and started to clean up. "I'd better go punch a few cows," he muttered, *and,* came his silent chide, *punch this green-eyed monster off my shoulder!*

CHAPTER FOUR

"Finally got them dang boys quieted down with another one of them vid-e-o movies. A good, solid Duke Wayne western. I hid that horror junk they wanted." With a chuckle, Nate eased his lean form into the other padded wooden rocker on the softly lit back porch.

He noisily sipped an oversized cup of brandy-enhanced coffee. "I never get tired of the changin' sunsets. Better than any vid-e-o or TeeVee. Mountains sure are pretty, glowin' pink and purple in what's left of the light. Oh, there go them bats. Hope they fill up on mosquitoes. The dang bugs are the size of the state bird."

Nate's brown eyes were almost hidden in the folds of a squint as he stared at Thor. "You're bein' mighty quiet. Can't recollect you sayin' more than three words at dinner."

"Two."

The foreman rubbed his jaw, the gray stubble of beard bending against the strength of a callused palm. "You sick, son?"

"Not sick. Exactly."

He pushed a fresh plug of chewing tobacco into the corner of his cheek. "Ain't sick, huh?" Nate rocked thoughtfully, chewing and squinting at Thor in the rapidly waning natural light. "My guess is you're plum cornfused, boy."

Thor smiled at the mispronunciation. "Yeah. Cornfused."

"A woman will do that to a man."

"Now wait just a darn minute," Thor retorted defensively. "Just what makes you think it's a woman and not—not ranch business or—or the boys or those rustlers?"

A high-pitched cackle splintered the shadows. " 'Cause the ranch, the boys, and them dang rustlers never shut you up! For that matter," Nate shifted the chaw in his mouth, *"women* have never shut you up. So, I figure it's got to be one particular woman. Like, say, that humdinger of a cat lady."

It was Thor's turn to rock.

Smiling, Nate listened to the rhythmic squeaks of his companion's chair. "Known you since you was born, son. Proud to say I helped raise ya'. Can't recall ever seein' you like this."

He aimed a stream of tobacco juice expertly into the aged brass spittoon by his feet. "Come to think of it, though, your dad acted right quiet when he met your mother. Quiet and squirrelly."

Nate laughed and slapped his knee. "Never will forget how fast Lucas turned from cowboy to greenhorn. Forgot to tighten his cinch strap, put his boot in the stirrup and his saddle slid clean off his horse. He landed slap-dab in the biggest puddle on Kalispell's rutted main street.

"We was quite a pair of young bucks back in forty-six. And Montana was wild and free. Lucas and me made a blood pact never to marry till we was old. At least thirty." He laughed again. "Trouble was your dad didn't count on meetin' Miz Nora at the annual rodeo. She was sellin' lemonade for a nickel a glass. Golden hair, sky blue eyes, and a smile like sunshine. Your ma rattled him. Lucas couldn't think. Couldn't work.

Couldn't talk. Yup, you're plum like your dad, all right."

Nate's voice grew deep and thoughtful. "Reckon even an old man of thirty-six could use his dad now an' again. Or his ma. A body could talk to Miz Nora 'bout anything." His sigh was heavy. "Sure do miss 'em. I curse every dang air-o-plane I see."

Each man became absorbed in his own memories. The only sounds that disturbed the night were the wind whispering around the corners and the creaking syncopation of the weathered rocking chairs. A distant owl hooted, followed by the soulful refrain of a coyote. Both seemed to serve as musical introductions to a chorus of crickets and cicadas.

Thor rested his head against the chair's high back. His eyes scanned the dark, star-dotted sky. The heavens were filled with shooting stars, meteors that flared bright before leaving a streak of light across the galaxy. A soft smile of remembrance curved his lips.

When he was a small boy, he had asked his mother about the stars. She'd told him they were souls. Some were to be babies, waiting in the heavens until they were called to earth. Some were the earthly departed, who had led such good lives that they were given a special reward.

And while Thor knew the truth about stars and meteors and babies and souls, a tiny part of him wanted to believe that two of the brightest stars were indeed his parents. Five years had passed since the airplane crash but his need for their wise council never subsided.

Thor stopped rocking, leaned forward, and placed his hand on Nate's arm. "Since I was lucky enough to have *two* fathers, perhaps you wouldn't mind letting me pick your brain about women."

Nate sniffed, spat, then grinned, his teeth flashing

briefly in the amber porch light. "You've come to the right man, son. Pick away."

"Ever been in love?"

"Lots of times. Plum loco nearly five."

"Why—why didn't you ever marry?" Thor inquired with unconcealed surprise. "You've always had your own place here on the ranch and a percentage of the profits."

"Yup, that is a fact."

"And as far as I can remember, you've never expressed an interest in leaving."

"Right again."

"Also, I've seen those old photos of you and Dad. You both were handsome men," Thor teased. "I don't think any lady would have said no."

Nate chuckled. "Never gave one a chance to throw a marriage offer back in my face."

"Well. . . ." He shook the foreman's knee. "You did say you'd been in love. Why no wife?"

" 'Cause the love weren't real. I didn't hurt here—" Nate's fist knocked his solar plexus. "That's where it struck your dad. That's the only place it counts." His tongue pushed the tobacco plug against his left cheek. "Besides, it takes a special kind of woman to live out here. Glacier country ain't no picnic grounds for the folks who work hard at ranchin'. Winter lasts into May, spring comes quick, summer goes even quicker. Remember last year? We had four inches of snow the first week of August."

Thor rocked his chair back and forth. "My mother never seemed to mind. She not only kept the house going but always helped with the calving and the foals. Even won at barrel riding in the yearly rodeo," he stated proudly.

"That's just the type of woman I was never able to locate," Nate commiserated. "You can tell a true fron-

70

tier-type woman. See it in her eyes. I found pretty 'nough eyes but the soul was missin'.''

Another stream of tobacco juice rang into the spittoon. "You know how I like readin' them pioneer stories. Well, I always remembered Daniel Boone's wife. Rebecca was her name. Old Dan Boone was the first to admit Rebecca could handle a Kentucky long rifle just as fine as he handled Tick-Licker. She kept the Indians at bay, farmed the land, and raised the kids, all while Dan was scoutin' the Wilderness Trail.

"Well, son, that story and that fine woman has stuck in my mind all these years. And that's the type of woman I was on the lookout for. A woman who was better than I was."

"A woman *better* than you?" Thor echoed.

"That's right, boy. That's the only kind of woman to marry, specially out here. You got to find one that don't need to eat in fancy restaurants, go shoppin' in fancy stores, or wear fancy duds. You need a woman who likes the quiet, the freedom, and the captivity. 'Cause, son, runnin' a ranch in Montana gives you all them things."

Thor nodded. "Quite true, Nate. It does take a special woman to make it out here."

"Your dad found one in Miz Nora. But I weren't as lucky. Came close a couple times but the second things got a little hard, pffft—" his hand sliced the air, "they'd up an' skedaddle. Made a man stop and think what would happen if the marriage fell on hard times."

Nate's chair creaked with metronomic tempo. "Interestin' to see how some people deal with harshities. Take that Bridget Lawson. She was afraid to do some runnin' yesterday, 'fraid to work up a sweat, 'fraid to get dirty. But not the cat lady. She's got what Duke Wayne had: true grit. No fear, neither. Didn't bat an eye when the rifles were aimed right at her." He spat again. "Can't say that I could have handled myself any better."

"Cam does know how to handle herself," Thor murmured reflectively. "I'm more fearful about her stunt work than she is."

"How's that, son?"

"Oh, nothing, Nate, just thinking out loud."

The foreman swirled what was left of his coffee in the mug. "That cat lady is grabbin' at your insides, ain't she?"

Thor's laugh was an embarrassed admission.

"Well, you might want to take a page out of your dad's courtin' book." Nate wiped his hand across his mouth. "Abstinence makin' the heart grow fonder. I remembered he tried stayin' clear of your ma for a while."

"It obviously didn't work."

"Nope. But I tried it on several occasions and it worked right fine."

Thor considered that option for a long moment, squared his shoulders, and announced, "Abstinence it is, Nate. Besides, there's that south pasture fence to mend."

"Already done."

"Oh. Hmm. Well, there's still that new colt to break."

"Buck did that." He spat again. "You'll be right glad to hear there ain't a broomtail in the herd."

"Okay, no fence, no colts . . . ah, I know, I'll get those weak boards in the barn loft replaced."

"The boys finished them today."

Thor cleared his throat. "Seems like I'll be *abstaining* from everything."

"No . . . now, there is one chore that's been sorely neglected."

"And which one's that?" Thor arched an expressive brow.

Nate's voice was even. "The laundry. Piles of it. We're all runnin' out of everything."

"The laundry?"

"You'll be settin' them boys a good example." Nate waved off a hungry mosquito. "Them dang bats ain't eatin' fast enough for me. And where's a nighthawk when you need 'em. Let's head inside, son, the coffee ain't cuttin' tonight's chill and I ain't gonna be fodder for these goll darn bugs."

"Laundry?"

Laughing, Nate clamped a hand on Thor's shoulder. "Just be glad you got two brand spankin' new washin' machines, son. Otherwise it'd be down to the pond with rocks and lye soap. And I can guaran-damn-tee that you'd be a scrubbin' till hell froze over!"

"I'm giving you a bonus when this picture is over."

"Can I have that in writing?"

"Why, Cam Stirling, don't you trust me?"

"Why, Jack Kenyon, if you get any closer to the edge you'll be given the Oscar posthumously and there goes my bonus!"

"Whoa!" Jack took more than a giant step backward. "That's the trouble with looking through a lens to check a shot, reality gets distorted." Wiping the top of his bald head with his Pirates' cap, he nodded to the scene below. "You sure this is safe for you, kid?"

"Would I do it if it wasn't?"

"No."

Cam's hand settled on his forearm. "We needed a waterfall and this one is perfect. It's a little over twenty-five feet high and has an exceptionally generous deep pool."

"Twenty-five feet? I don't know, Cam, it looks and sounds twice that size."

"That's one reason I chose it over the other waterfalls

in the area." She led him back to the edge, her voice growing in volume to cover the din of the water. "Twenty-five feet is the regulation height of a practice platform dive. And the pool . . . well, I couldn't believe my luck, it's close to thirteen feet deep. The force of the water runoff adds more protection.

"Look at the terrain, Jack. This is a damn close match to the white-water stream footage we shot in Idaho. Spruce and fir trees, even the rock formations ring familiar and . . . watch the water."

Jack peered through the viewfinder, adjusting the zoom lens for a close-up inspection. "Hmm, you know, kid, I think you're right. Especially about the way the white water crashes down between those black rocks. I'll have an easy time with the splicing. Only minimal use of optical printers and computers."

His mouth twisted from delight to concern. "But what about all those very pretty pink and gray stones? And the depth? Granted, that crater pool appears deep, but I—well, I . . ."

"I don't want a broken neck either," Cam returned. "I'm going to spend what's left of the afternoon relocating those rocks and digging the crater deeper." She gave Jack an easy smile. "Then I'll be able to give you a nice vertical dive. Body straight, toes pointed, arms extended. Should look great."

"Sounds Olympic gold medal class."

"Believe me, it's going to be the proverbial piece of cake compared to the Class IV rapids between the Impassable Canyon of the Salmon River."

"Now, now, the first one hundred miles was only swift water," came Jack's teasing reminder as they walked back to quieter, safer, and less soggy ground. "The scenery was incredible. The water was so clear that . . . well, we had to edit all those trout that showed up in the rushes."

74

"Say, what's with the sudden frown? You just said how great it looked."

Jack's fingers scratched his black bush of a beard. "True, true. I just wish we could have used the Grand Canyon. I'm still thinking of shooting some footage of the Vishnu and splicing it in. Those ancient rocks are two billion years old and you can see the layers of the earth. That, coupled with the prehistoric atmosphere of this area plus special effects, will make the movie-going public goggle-eyed." He rubbed his hands together. "That's my favorite effect."

"And your favorite result is money," she said with a grin.

"That too! Why are you looking so dreamy eyed?"

"I was just remembering the nice benefit of the natural hot springs near our campsite in Idaho." Cam's sigh was long and exaggerated. "I could sure use a hot tub most nights."

"Solar showers are as far as my budget will stretch. Of course, you might ask," Jack's eyes narrowed, his voice turned coy, "your Mr. Luthor Devlin if he has a hot tub available."

"*My* Mr. Devlin?"

Jack laughed and wagged a peremptory finger at her. "Innocence does become you, Camilla. Darrell's been telling the strawberry story for the last two days."

"With embellishment, I gather."

"Whipped cream and cherries." His manner turned protectively parental. "I know you dared Devlin for the sake of production but you don't have to keep up a pretense and—"

"I didn't *have* to from the beginning," she returned matter-of-factly. Cam stared past Jack, her eyes focusing on clouds that drifted like cotton batting. "I wanted to see him again. But that was two days, three hours, and a handful of minutes ago. So," she blinked quickly, took a deep breath and smiled, "maybe the strawberry story was my finale."

Jack pretended great interest in his mud-covered canvas boat shoes. "I've known you for ten years, Cam. Through movies and television, big productions and small, we've yelled at each other, partied with each other, cheered and jeered each other."

Swallowing hard, he looked up at her. "I know your background and your strong ideals. And for all the time I've known you, respected you, trusted in you, well, this is the first time I can ever recall you wanting an involvement."

His upright palm stalled her protest. "Please, innocence becomes you, lying doesn't. I can see it in your eyes, even if I do have to stand on my tiptoes."

She laughed and shook her head. "You're right. This is different. Or was. Maybe my planets are out of alignment or my karma's out of whack."

"Or maybe they're all finally in place . . . at the right time . . . with the right person."

"A romantic? You, Jack?"

"Don't I always promise your folks and those three burly brothers of yours to keep a watchful eye on you?"

"That promise is in the area of hazardous stunt work," she reminded him. "Besides, I think a man working on his third divorce at age, um, forty should train his watchful eyes on himself."

"Ouch! I am wounded."

"The only thing that wounds you is the size of your monthly alimony checks. Ah . . . saved by the helicopter." Hands on Jack's shoulders, Cam quickstep marched him down the cliff's rutted path. She was laughing, he perspiring and out of breath by the time they reached the bottom. "I think you should requisition yourself hazard pay."

Jack gulped for air, his hand splayed against the front

76

of his sweat-stained T-shirt. "I'm . . . going . . . to . . . requisition . . . a cold . . . beer!" Leaning against the chopper's tail boom, he watched Cam and the pilot pull diving gear, tools, and a green plastic picnic cooler from the cockpit. "Got everything you're going to need?"

"Even the walkie-talkie." She patted the compact radio transmitter and receiver hooked to the belt loop on her jeans. "With the tanks empty, I'll be able to haul everything back on my horse when I finish up."

Jack glanced at the smooth-backed, deep-chested black gelding grazing under a triangular pocket of aspen. "Better you on that horse than me. I prefer mechanical beasts." He patted the helicopter. "At least I won't get trampled."

"Zodiac's better trained than Lassie!"

"I know. Why do you think I hired your horse? He's just big!" Jack shivered. "Okay, let's just double-check your gear and . . . say, what's this note taped to the basket?" He pulled the paper free. "Darrell requests that you wear the enclosed bathing suit and get plenty of sun. Seems you're pale next to Bridget." His grin was lopsided. "Colorwise only, kid."

Jack straightened to his full Napoleonic height. "Now, listen, if you need any help, we're just a call away. I know I've got the stunt men and the extras booked this afternoon but I can always manage to free up somebody."

"I'm not going to do anything stupid. And I won't be taking any practice dives until someone's around. But I would like to get at least one in today," she added.

"Okay. I'll have the chopper bring me back here around, um, four but I'll still be giving you a squawk every two hours."

"Thanks, Dad." She patted his cheek.

"Get me the hell out of here, Hank!" Jack jerked a

thumb at the pilot, then jumped into the passenger's seat.

The ginlike smell of Rocky Mountain juniper pellets together with sprigs of aromatic sage and goldenrod chased the acrid fumes of laundry detergent and bleach from Thor's nostrils. He stretched, tall in the saddle, relishing the privacy, solitude, and beauty of this very different corner of his land.

Whereas the escarpment was primal, forbidding, and morose, this pocket was radiant, reassuring, and full of life. Even Pegasus stepped carefully around the blue asters and columbines that preened in the sun, as if loath to let his hooves ruin the landscape.

But it was more than the comforting, earthy fragrances of sweet grasses and wild huckleberries that guided Thor. He angled the stallion toward a private place where he'd always come to sort out confused feelings. Even from a distance, the roar of cascading water and the remembered image of a crystal plunge pool cleansed and soothed him.

Abstinence. Absence. Work. Whatever. Nothing had made Thor's heart less fonder. Especially at night. When he was alone. In the dark. In bed.

Cam Stirling became more potent, more sensual, more haunting. And Thor became a man in want, in need, inflamed. To his eyes the shadows shaped her heightened image. His ears tingled with her laughter. His mouth tasted her ripe lips. His fingers burned to touch her silken skin. It proved sweet torture, one that entertained his body, mind, and soul.

Two days was more than he could handle. The memory of the time with her overshadowed everything and everyone else. When he went back to the escarpment, he'd found nothing. Just gloom, doom, and natural fog. Thor had spent the morning scouting for the movie company, finally locating them in the valley. He didn't need to use binoculars to see that the empress was Bridget and not Cam. A weak, comic-book cutie couldn't be disguised as the real thing. But the real thing was not to be found.

Pegasus' sudden fractious behavior put Thor on alert. The stallion snorted, pawed, and nickered. "Take it easy, boy." Thor's hand soothed the buckskin's neck. "I don't see or hear anything."

The horse issued a fevered whinny and, despite strong reining, discharged a mule kick. An answering neigh directed Thor's attention to a stand of aspen and Engelmann spruce. The animal that pranced into view had both rider and horse backing up in surprise.

"Movie tricks!" Thor consoled Pegasus. "If not, we've discovered the eighth wonder of the world. A unicorn. With a gold horn and wings." Dismounting, he cautiously walked toward the large black gelding.

The unicorn proved friendly and anxious for company. Its contented whinny was followed by a playful nudge that dislodged the horn, sending it tumbling into Thor's hand. "Ah, how quickly fantasy becomes reality." He massaged the horse's muzzle. "Now, we're both in trouble. Let's go face the music."

Horses in tow, he strode into the clearing. Thor expected to be confronted by a raging Jack Kenyon or the simpering, nasal tones of Darrell Booth. But he discovered neither. Actually, at first glance, he found nothing but what Nature intended: a thundering cascade of glacier water, a large, clear plunge pool, and stunning rock formations, all surrounded by lush mountain vegetation.

It was the black gelding's artistic scampering that drew his attention to a limestone scree. There, neatly piled on the lichened boulders, were clothes. Thor politely set to one side a white cotton bra and briefs to unfold faded jeans. Their small waist and slim cut infused hope. And when the red T-shirt revealed the name *Stirling* stenciled across the back, Thor's broad grin went beyond hope to relief.

"Cam! Cam!" Hat pushed back, hands on hips, Thor listened and waited but received no reply. Well, she had to come back sometime, so he'd just relax and . . . What was this camouflaged between the rocks? A picnic cooler. He flipped down the molded plastic handle to peer inside. It was filled to the brim with more than enough for two and something for the horses as well. His fingers curled around a bunch of carrots.

Half an hour later, the horses had polished off the carrots and were happily munching tussocky grass while Thor was lying, half asleep, in a lush bed of delphiniums and elkhorn. A sassy ground squirrel jabbered his intentions of purloining the crumbs on the paper plates while a snowshoe rabbit in summer-brown fur quietly made a meal of new green shoots.

A flutter of wings and violent honking caused Thor to roll on his side and look toward the water. The trio of ducks he'd been feeding had abandoned their swimming. Disturbed by what? All was silent, quiet and . . . Bubbles erupted on the calm outer perimeter of the pool, percolating, then boiling before splitting apart to allow a diver to surface.

Thor quickly moved to the water's edge. "First a unicorn, now a nymph." Cam tossed her mask and a small shovel at him. His tongue clicked against the roof of his mouth as he watched her free herself from the regulator and air tank. "Hmm, I never realized naiads wore hot pink bikinis. Then again, they are supposed to inspire us mortals."

Her slightly breathless voice had nothing to do with diving. "We twenty-third-century nymphs are under the direct inspiration of our makeup directors." Her hand checked the security of the bandeau bra top. "Darrell ordered me to tan." Calmer and curious, she favored Thor with a wet, wide smile. "Nice to see you again."

"Ah, you missed me."

Cam avoided the directness of his words and the boldness of his eyes. "But I can see you didn't miss my lunch."

"There's plenty left unless that pesky squirrel climbed into the cooler. What on earth have you been doing under there?"

She squeezed the excess water from her braided hair. "Digging the crater where the cascade hits a little deeper and wider and moving about a half-dozen small rocks. Tiring and hungry work."

Stepping closer, Thor's arm circled her damp shoulders and, the instant contact was made, he felt content. "Allow me to escort you to what's left of your lunch."

"Thank you, kind sir." She hoped the sigh that abruptly escaped would be taken for weariness. Cam, however, knew the truth of its origin. Happiness. And it had taken only an instant to reignite the magic.

But it was important for her to know that the magic was real and that it worked both ways. *Cautious and careful,* her conscience warned. She decided a slow foray into each other's personalities was the way to proceed and really know if the vibrations were positive. Maybe even permanent.

He handed her a roast beef sandwich and opened a bottle of lime mineral water. "Why were you digging the crater?"

"Because I'm diving off the top ledge of the falls and needed a bit more depth." Cam was struggling to open a packet of ketchup. "Here. Fingertips like shriveled prunes are utterly worthless." She squinted at his odd expression. "Don't tell me these plastic things defeat you too?"

He ran a hand through his hair. "Not these. You."

"Me? Why?"

"Because you're sitting here, wearing two pink ribbons of frankly feminine attire and," his voice deepened, "looking agonizingly sexy and in the sweetest, most nonchalant tone I've ever heard, calmly saying, 'I'm going to jump off a waterfall'!" Thor inhaled deeply, then continued in a quick, higher tone, "And I just can't understand why a perfectly sane, intelligent, witty, wonderful woman would—would . . ."

"Die for a living?"

"Yes—yes! Die for a living." He felt something warm and wet in his palm and groaned. "Aw, hell, here's your ketchup."

Cam took a napkin and began wiping the red sauce from his fingers and hand. "Can I ask you something?"

"What's that?"

It was difficult not to smile at the gruffness of his words. "Why are you a rancher and not a civil engineer? I told you I did see a degree."

Thor flexed his cleaned hand. "I worked at being an engineer for four years. Went all over the world building bridges and dams, then came back and put in a year of desktop design."

He cleared his throat, relaxing somewhat under the easy rapport that accompanied their talks. "But I began to view each workday as a penance. Not that the job wasn't interesting or challenging. I just—well, my mind would always drift back to the ranch. I was calling my folks every night, asking about the stock, land problems . . . hell, I just wasn't happy in the city or with a nine-to-five job or with the thought that one day I'd wake up and be a career coffee drinker."

"We're a lot alike," she returned easily. "I was a practicing physical therapist. Seems we both gave up nice, sensible careers to do something that's, well, ingrained in our psyches."

His eyes widened. "You're comparing apples and oranges, Cam. Running a ranch in Montana is not the same as jumping off a waterfall. Why do you tempt the fates? Is it—hell, I don't know. . . ." Thor scratched his cheek, averting his eyes "Is it this woman's liberation thing? Some suicidal urge? Does fear excite you?"

"Fear is not one of my problems."

"That's one helluva cocky statement."

Cam ran a hand over her face and tried to put her thoughts in order. "I don't get any sexual gratification from jumping a waterfall. And I don't have any suicidal urges." She leaned forward and winked. "I'm murderous sometimes when directors act crazy but never self-destructive.

"You know, thinking about it, stunt work is very close to engineering. We carefully calculate hazards and possible consequences. I'm not a daredevil but an illusionist. Every stunt takes agility, timing, and practice. It's an exact science, nothing is left to chance." Her hand settled briefly on his arm. "I'm not in this business to die."

"Have you ever been hurt?"

"I once broke both my feet and legs—"

"Ah, ah . . ."

"Taking out the garbage. My brother left his skateboard in the middle of the driveway. True, the injury factor in stunt work is certainly there but you just can't dwell on it. In fact, injuries abound everywhere and in every occupation." She arched a curious brow. "What about you, Mr. Devlin? Any ranching accidents?"

"Well, you know . . ." he coughed, cleared his throat, and coughed again.

"Ah, ah . . ."

"Eat your sandwich." Thor smiled at her teasing laughter. "How long have you been doing stunt work?"

"Hmm," Cam munched thoughtfully, "well, I had my first job on a TV series when I was two."

"Two years old? As in twenty-four months?"

"Yup. I was hit by a car on one of those detective shows."

"Your parents allowed this?"

"My father was driving the car." Her lips twisted. "Did I forget to tell you that my entire family are stunt people? Even my grandmothers." Cam bit into a pickle. "The *L.A. Times* did an article about us a few years ago when we were all working on the same picture together. The reporter called us twentieth-century gladiators."

"Are you?"

"In a way, we do entertain spectators. But frankly, I'm just your basic model woman. Happy, sad, simple, complex, confident, confused, outgoing, shy, and," she wiggled her fingers, "sticky."

Thor grinned. "That makes two of us." He followed her to the pool. The surface looked sequined in sunshine. "You picked a very special waterfall for your dive."

"How's that?"

"According to legend, this is one of the falls used by Pitamakan."

"And who is Pitamakan?"

"Her white man's name was Running Eagle and there's a waterfall of the same name in Two Medicine Valley on the southeast side. Anyway, Pitamakan was a great warrior woman who fought alongside the wildly feared and respected Blackfeet men. She sought visions of battles in the falls and power from the surrounding mountains. When the vision showed victory, Pitamakan would lead a band of Blackfeet warriors on a raid for Sioux ponies."

Cam's body vibrated under the deep, husky baritone of Thor's voice as he added, "You're a lot like Pitamakan. Fearless. Brave. Beautiful. While I won't pretend to understand what you do or why you do it, I can see it makes you happy and I do know how important that is to a person's mental health."

Their fingers played in the water, moving closer and closer together until they met and interlocked.

Cam wondered if she should stick her neck out and take a risk. Not her usual physical type but a more powerful, emotional risk. Like Pitamakan, her gaze sought a vision in the pool. The only image reflected there were a pair of coupled hands. The vision shimmered deep, and she decided she wasn't afraid to tell Thor how much she cared.

"Yes." Her suddenly spoken word surprised him. "To the very first question you asked me. I did miss you. The missing grew stronger every minute of the last two days."

His blue eyes locked into hers. "For me too. I spent the morning trying to hunt you down. Finally found the movie set, but no you. Just a lot of explosions and flying Neanderthal men, trumpeting pseudomammoths, and a snarling saber-toothed tiger."

Thor lifted their hands out of the water and placed them against his chest. The rapid beating of his heart thrilled her palm. She felt warm, alive, and an intense need to connect.

"I never realized just how empty my life was until you wandered in." He leaned forward, his left arm wrapping tightly around her slim waist. "Luck and chance threw us together and I don't think it'd be a good idea to ignore fate." Thor's gaze focused on her half-parted lips. "Let's just help it along."

His mouth slanted hungrily over hers, making her breath part of his own. Her lips and body welcomed him. Her full breasts pressed tight against his broad chest.

Cam knew only satisfaction as her fingers moved along his nape, reveling in the thick, virile curls. He tried to control the urgency that again propelled his every movement. But the touch and the taste of her were potent aphrodisiacs that fueled his heightened senses.

Thor gently pushed her backward into the thick, sweet grass. She anxiously pulled him on top of her, loath to have anything separate them. His eager mouth rained possessive kisses over her face, neck, and the curve of her shoulder. His tongue sampled her damp skin, his lips moving greedily along the swells of her breast.

Her fingers tugged his shirt free of his belted jeans, her hands roaming languidly over his sinewy back, her fingernails drawing teasing, erotic patterns on his spine. She couldn't seem to get close enough to him.

His mouth captured and savored her lips while his fingers displaced the scant bra top on her bikini. His hands grew bolder and more possessive as they shaped the soft, generous curves of her breasts. His knuckle awakened a shy nipple, his lips and tongue proved the sensual catalyst that brought it to erect delight.

"You feel like silk and taste like heady wine." Thor kissed her again, taking his time. A pleasurable sigh escaped her as the callused tips of his fingers toyed with her hardened nipples.

Her body seemed to conspire with his. Her hands lovingly explored the rugged landscape of his body, enjoying his low moans of delight.

But it was a louder, longer, mournful moan that drew them apart, a moan coupled with playful splashing. A black bear with two cubs, one deep brown, one rust, had wandered into their private oasis.

"Take it easy," Thor whispered. "You don't want to scare a grizzly; you just let them know you're here."

"Us scare them?" Cam struggled to her knees, re-aligning her top. "Where's your gun?"

"On my saddle."

"Great place for it." Cam watched the mother bear stop and press her nose in a rotted log, her claws sweeping aside a clot of mud. "Now what's she doing?"

"Looking for grubs. Probably lunchtime." He positioned himself protectively in front of Cam. "Why don't you quietly back toward the horses—"

"They've wandered off. I can whistle for mine and yours will probably follow."

Suddenly the bear whuffed and reared. Her black shaggy head turned, her muzzle working in the wind. She bleated, dropped back onto her front feet, and headed into the aspen forest, her cubs scurrying quickly behind.

"I'm sure glad she's gone," Cam wrapped her arms around Thor's waist, her face resting on his back. "I wonder if something bigger scared her away."

"Listen." He pointed skyward and made a face. "Helicopter."

"I bet it's Jack or some of the stunt men coming to see how I'm doing."

His finger settled perfectly in the cleft of her chin. "You and I were doing just fine." He gave her a quick, hard kiss. "You're blushing again."

"So are you."

Thor stared into Cam's eyes and realized he was more than a little bit in love—and in love with a woman who was better than he was. Ninety-nine percent of him was thrilled.

CHAPTER FIVE

"No, no, the work's going fine here. Been raining all day; you can guess what kind of mood Kenyon's in—" A sharp rap on the trailer door interrupted Cam's phone call. "Come in." She was surprised when Bridget's peach raincoated figure sidled into the room. "Well, I'm glad the boys landed work in that new MGM movie. Okay, you two take care of yourselves. Bye . . . bye."

Cradling the receiver, Cam watched Bridget lift dainty bare feet from oversized duck boots. "I was just talking to my grandmothers. They're practicing running each other over with a truck. They've got a TV gig next month." She motioned for the actress to join her on the plaid minidivan. "What's up?"

"Oh, I was bored listening to the rain's chainlike sonata on the metal roof of my Airstream, so I thought I'd visit the major source of gossip on this movie set." Bridget's thickly mascaraed left lash closed in a slow, sly wink. "Inquiring minds want to know."

"Know what?"

"Everything." Drawing her legs underneath her, she leaned forward, her spirits exhilarated. "Come on, Cam, we've known each other for five years. Fess up, there was obviously an initial attraction between you and Mr. Devlin, or he would have sent us all packing.

Then there was that breakfast and the strawberry/cleavage story Darrell's been spreading. And yesterday—"

Cam sighed. "What about yesterday?"

Bridget brushed invisible lint from the V neck of her silk Picasso-print jumpsuit. "The chopper pilot, Hank —well, I overheard him telling one of the key grips something about you and Devlin and bare bodies."

"That's *b-e-a-r*, as in grizzly," she returned. "Damn! And men have the nerve to say women gossip!"

"I've worked with Darrell Booth before," the actress related as she lit up a gold-tipped monogrammed designer cigarette. "He is positively the biggest tattletale in the industry. I hear he sells information to those supermarket tabloids." Her lips formed a fuchsia frame around a white puff of smoke. "Do you mean all those rumors about you and Mr. Devlin are nothing but hot air?"

"I suppose I could lie and say yes."

"Oh . . . ohhhh . . ."

"You're smiling again, Bridget."

"So are you, Camilla." Cigarette bobbing in her mouth, she rubbed her palms together. "Okay, let's get down and dirty. What's happening with you and the handsome rancher?"

"I'm not really sure. Something. Nothing. Everything."

"Lack of experience," Bridget diagnosed.

"I work with men every day."

"Work with, yes, but that's not the same. You only deal with men on a surface, business level. Purely pseudoemotional and—" Suddenly she laughed at Cam's expression. "Just because I have blow-dried hair does not mean I have blow-dried brains. I know what the industry thinks of me. Just boobs and buns, the old T & A.

"I had one director actually tell me I was only hired for my body and to pretend I was human. And, since you're too polite to ask, I have indeed used my body to get ahead. You know the big difference between you and me, Cam? Principles. I lost mine years ago on the proverbial casting couch."

"Principles are easily restored."

Bridget's blue eyes grew narrow behind their smoky veil, her voice thinned. "If you want them. Right now, I'm exploiting my own assets. Since I know where, how, and with whom, I'm in control."

She inhaled a lungful of smoke. "You know, Cam, some men are damn decent. They're tough to find. Others, well, they treat a woman like she's nothing more than sex organs. So far, beauty's been enough for me. Except for some nights when I'm all alone, then it's not."

Cam stared at the actress for a long moment. "I—I wouldn't have thought you'd spend any evenings alone. You're widely photographed with a new man on your arm for every party. You have your pick of all those men—"

"It's not *all those men* I want. Just one particular, special understanding man will do. And do very nicely. All those men? They're studio requisitions or agent setups. Frankly, girl, ninety percent of them are mental midgets, or not interested in women, or suspect in areas too numerous to mention."

Their unison sigh of regret had them both laughing.

"Ever been married, Bridget?"

"No. You?"

"No."

Another designer cigarette was flamed to life. "Any live-ins?"

"No. As a matter of fact, I live in a family compound.

Have my own wing, but my folks, grandmothers, and three brothers are there too."

"That's really nice. My mother always said a decent girl gets married from her home. Of course, my mother's been married from her home six times."

Cam watched six perfect smoke rings float up and out the trailer's air conditioning vent. "Want a soda?"

"Anything diet."

She reached down, opened the tiny refrigerator, and pulled two colas from the door tray. Cam handed one to Bridget. "What you said before, about men viewing women as sex objects? That's not my problem."

It was Bridget's turn to be surprised. "Hell, you look like my twin! Frankly, between you and me, you've got a better bod. But I'll rip out your throat if you ever tell anyone I said that." She carefully snapped the tab opener and sipped at the soda. "So, what is your problem?"

"A rather unique life-style." Cam's fingernail drew random designs amid the condensation on the can. "I either attract a weak man who's looking for a strong mother figure—that's happened twice," she shivered in remembrance. "You know, Bridget, they look perfectly normal but within a couple of hours . . ."

"I *do* know—they need to be burped, diapered, and fed." Her lips twisted in a sneer. "I had my share of the weak ones too. Unfortunately, it took me longer than a couple of hours to figure them out."

Cam slid down on her spine. "The other thing I run into with men is that after an initial phase of fascination and awe, they feel threatened."

"Welcome to the club, girl! A movie star," her fingers wiggled around the invisible word, "well, that's a tough title for a man to handle. Plus, Hollywood society is very clannish and insular; it's hard to break in, even tougher if the person's an outsider."

Bridget lit another cigarette. "But listen, Cam, if all those articles I read in the women's magazines and newspapers are true, then threatened men are the norm now that women are moving into high-powered positions. Women executives, lawyers, doctors, et cetera all have to deal with that.

"Today, it's the men who have to change; they're the ones who have to do the fitting in a relationship because no woman I know is going to abandon her career until it abandons her. Now why are you shaking your head?"

"I agree with you, Bridget, but that's not the threatening I meant." Cam pulled up her legs, resting her chin on denim-covered knees. "Even in today's so-called age of enlightenment the self-image of many men still depends on their careers, the heft of their wallets, and the size of their muscles. We both can knock them on the first two, but I also deliver a sizable punch on the last."

"I don't suppose there are many men who can do what you do. Or who want to do what you do," Bridget commiserated. "So, I guess it would grate some macho types—"

"All men are macho types," Cam interjected. "Even the sensitive, liberated ones. Sometimes I wonder if I'm holding an unrealistic expectation for men's attitudes. Then I remember how it never seems to bother a man when a woman can cook and clean better than they can.

"But just let one of us jump off a building, total a car, shoot a gun, throw a punch, or do trick riding and what happens? Mr. Macho can't compete, turns tail, and runs." She frowned at her T-shirt and jeans and straightened her posture. "Maybe I'm not feminine enough, maybe—"

"Don't be silly! You're very feminine and very attractive—remember, you could be my twin. Besides, I've seen you get shot and fall down a flight of stairs in an

Oscar de la Renta gown and Tiffany jewels. If that's not feminine, I don't know what else is!"

Cam opened her mouth, closed it, then started to laugh. The actress quickly joined her.

"You know what I mean," Bridget retorted. She let a mouthful of soda wash away her embarrassment. "What about Devlin's reaction to your work? He seems to be running toward you, not away."

"Am I getting a goofy, lovesick expression on my face?"

"You certainly are, Camilla."

"Well, he's really concerned about my safety."

"Haven't you told him that you are known around the industry as Miz Safety Stunt?"

"I didn't know that!"

Bridget laughed. "Liar! I'll never forget when you told that snot of a TV director to do something anatomically impossible to himself when he wanted you to do a fire stunt on that cop show I was doing."

"His version of protection and my version left a lot of third-degree burns in between."

"So, Devlin's concerned about you. That's a good sign." She peered at Cam through the high yellow flame on her disposable lighter. "As I recall, the size of that man's muscles looked pretty healthy."

"They feel pretty healthy too."

"Oooooh, Camilla!" Bridget grinned. "That a girl, take dead aim and—"

"Things seem to be moving way too fast. Isn't love supposed to be slow and steady?"

"I tried it slow and steady," the actress responded, her expression serious. "Tried it three times. Wasted a total of nine years. Luckily I escaped any palimony suits. My new motto is: If it feels right, go for it! So far I haven't met anyone that feels right. But then I didn't get to the hunky Mr. Devlin first." Bridget cocked her head. "I know you, Cam, you never get involved when you're working. This man must have made a dynamite first impression."

"He did. And he keeps impressing me. He's very secure in himself, confident, witty, yet self-effacing." Her sigh was more than dreamy. "You know, Bridget, I become very content and happy whenever I'm with him." *And feel very sexy and womanly,* she added silently.

"Take my advice and go for him, Cam. Let your hormones and heart overrule your head. You—" The actress was interrupted by pounding on the trailer door.

"Hey, Cam—" Brad Owens, one of the stunt men, poked his rugged face inside. "Howdy, Miss Lawson." He nodded politely. "Cam, now that the rain's stopped, we're heading into town for some greasy pizza, cold beer, and an early movie. The local paper says they're running the sci-fi monster movie we all worked on two years ago. Wanna come?"

"Go ahead, Cam," Bridget stretched off the divan. "I'm going to soak in a hot tub, call the masseur, and wait for my gourmet meal to arrive." Her mischievous wink belied her affected tone. "I need some champagne to cleanse the diet soda taste from my mouth."

"I don't know how you stand working with that smug dame," Brad grumbled once Bridget had pushed her way out of the trailer.

"She's really not that bad," Cam said, stepping behind an open closet door to exchange her T-shirt for a soft white sleeveless sweater. She ran a hasty comb through her hair and grabbed her purse. "Okay, let's go before Mother Nature decides to drench us again."

"Weather report says all clear." He tossed Cam her suede jacket. "You'll need this, kiddo, it'll be cold driving back in an open jeep."

* * *

"I can't believe you guys!" Cam pushed her way through the clustered group of five burly stunt men. "I have never been so embarrassed in my life!"

"Wait a minute, wait a minute!" Brad ran in front of her, turned and walked backward. "The manager only yelled at us three times."

Stopping abruptly in the lobby of the theater, she caused a four-body pileup behind her. "Only three times? I counted five. One for each of you lugs and the last was a threat to call the police." Cam shook her head and found herself showered by popcorn. "Babies! You should all go back inside and pick up every thrown kernel."

"Nag, nag, nag!" Brad grabbed her elbow and nodded to the man behind her.

"Bitch, bitch, bitch!" Len Traynor grabbed Cam's other elbow and together the two men lifted her off the ground, out the theater's glass doors, and down two blocks to the pizza parlor.

It was a jubilant, laughing group that pushed inside the restaurant but the pizzeria's dark, silent interior quelled the raucous party.

"Well, boys, I guess four-thirty on Thursday is not pizza time in Montana." Hands on hips, Cam wandered around the empty dining room. "Place looks good enough. Big soup and salad bar."

"And there's a jukebox here that's hungry for quarters," Brad added. "Come on, let's push a few tables together and—"

Cam hissed, "On your best behavior, guys, the kitchen door just swung open." She smiled pleasantly at the startled young waitress. "Hope you're open for business."

"Ah, yes, just. I thought you were—I was expecting —oh, well, let me show you to a table—"

"We can handle the tables, Jennifer," Brad's finger tapped the nameplate on her white uniform.

"Oh, well, I'll—I'll," her fingers nervously played with her dark ponytail, "get menus."

"No need for that either," Brad continued over the din of scraping chair and table legs. "We'd like six of your big thick pan pizzas with everything, including anchovies. Salads all around. And six pitchers of your best draft beer. Plus a mug of cola for her," he jerked a thumb at Cam. "She's our designated driver, so she won't be drinking."

"Don't worry, the guys are perfectly harmless and I'll be sure to keep them in line," Cam quickly interjected, trying to calm the young woman's obvious consternation. "Is it usually this quiet around here?"

"Fridays and Saturdays are our big nights but I've got a party of twelve coming in two hours—"

"We'll be staying longer than that, honey," Brad told the flustered waitress, then yelled, "Guys, video and pinball machines at two o'clock."

"Oh, dear, I better call and get some help." Jennifer mumbled all the way back to the kitchen with an occasional over-the-shoulder peek at Brad.

Cam folded her arms across her chest. "You scared her."

Brad laughed. "My handsome face and rakish grin never scare women, just turn them on." He pushed his face nose to nose with hers. "I don't scare you." When music blasted forth, he pulled her hands free. "Dance with me, Cam."

She playfully tugged a handful of ebony hair. "I'm scared now, Mr. Two Left Feet!"

Two hours later, five pizzas, four salads, seven pitchers of beer, and four mugs of soda had been consumed. The video machines and jukebox fell silent in deference to six finally satiated bodies who were busily pursuing a quieter pastime.

Brad cleared his throat. "Okay, boys and girl, the last card is down and dirty." His practiced hands quickly dealt a round of playing cards. "Okay, um, Len, you're up."

"Check." His dark eyes shifted left. "Cam?"

"Hmm, I'll open for thir—"

"Cam! You're not supposed to eat the poker chips!"

"The pepperoni's good. Besides," her lashes fluttered guilefully, "I've got so many more than everyone else." A chorus of masculine groans assaulted Cam as she tossed a baker's dozen of pepperoni slices into a dish centered on the table. "That'll be a good start."

"Fold."

"Fold."

"Same."

"Out."

"Me too."

Her mouth twisted. "You guys aren't any fun. Of course you did add to my edible chips." Cam pulled the dish toward her. "Who's got the deal?"

"No more deals," Len stated. "I'm headin' for a showdown with the Avenger pinball machine." He patted his stomach. "Got to work this off before I tackle more food. Anyone else coming?"

Three additional chairs were scraped back, leaving Cam to stare at Brad. "How about blackjack?"

He shook his head. "How about another run on the dance floor? I've got to practice, get a little smoother." At her quizzical expression, Brad added, "Did I forget to tell you I'm doing a dance floor stunt on that new TV miniseries?"

"You certainly did." She stood up, stretched, and followed him to the jukebox. "The guys are headed to South Carolina to work on a drive-in B movie. I guess

I'm the only one unemployed once this job's finished. What are you playing?"

"An old BeeGees' disco tune. We danced to this in that Travolta movie." The pulsating beat and smooth lyrics surmounted the beeps and bongs coming from the video corner.

Cam's body moved naturally to the rhythm and easily followed Brad's leading moves. But intricate dance steps soon gave way to sillier choreography. Glides and slides, swings and sways, dipping and whirling, laughing and twirling—all with dizzying intensity.

It was on a multi-revolving, high-speed spin, that Cam broke the security of Brad's hand. Reeling across the dance floor, she slammed into something very solid and very breathing. Her ears registered a startled grunt, and the masculine arms that circled and steadied her felt oddly familiar.

Cam's eyes struggled open, diligently trying to bring a triple image into single focus. A youthful, excited voice shattered her concentration.

"Guys, look! It's the naked lady from the mountain!" A freckled, red-hair-topped face peered at Cam. "Hey, where's your tiger?"

"Billy!" Thor's voice was low and controlled.

"Sorry, Mr. Devlin." Billy's irrepressible grin belied his sober tone. He gawked at the hulking stunt men. "Oh, wow, there's more movie people."

Brad pushed his way through the clustered, chattering boys. "You okay, Cam?"

"Fine. If that's your stunt, it's not perfected. You need a—" her fingers moved from rubbing her forehead to cover Thor's hand at her waist "—catcher." She grinned at Thor. "Wanna be a stunt man?"

"I'll stick to ranching." His hand tightened possessively against the soft knit of her sweater.

Billy led a protest of "aws" that sent Nate into action. The foreman herded the teenagers toward the rear booths, but the boys made a sharp detour to the game area. Brad nodded to Thor, mumbled another apology to Cam, then drifted off to join the others.

Thor's fingertips gently brushed aside the blond curls that tumbled on her cheek. "Are you sure you're all right?" He carefully inspected every inch of her up-turned face.

"Feeling better and better." His slow smile caused a delightful giddiness to pepper her body. "Brad got a little rambunctious. And from the sounds of it, the whole group is getting carried away."

She peered over Thor's shoulder. "We came into town for some instant civilization but I guess you can't take the Neanderthal out of those guys. Seems the perfect rowdy match."

"The boys were antsy, the rain was boring, Nate and I brought them in for a movie and food. I missed being with you today."

Cam blinked twice, her attention wholly focused on the man standing in front of her.

"I missed talking to you, holding you, touching you. And I'm exercising supreme self-control right this minute because—damn, I want to kiss you."

The movement of his sensual mouth and the husky timbre of his voice were rapidly seducing her. She leaned toward him. Her fingers locked around his denim belt loops while her lips parted in anticipation. But wild whooping from the video machines dampened Cam's response. "The boys are restless."

"You cast a strange spell, Cam Stirling, you made me forget all about them."

His half-hooded eyes and lopsided smile made her feel quite weak. "The effect is very mutual, Mr. Devlin."

"Seems we're never alone." He rubbed his jaw. "Five

minutes. Five *private* minutes. Someplace quiet. With you. But that's asking the impossible with this crew," came his realistic appraisal.

"Maybe not."

"You've got an idea?"

"Could be."

"Tell me." Thor groaned. "When you grin like that, the cutest dimple forms in your right cheek and I want to—"

Billy materialized, as if by magic, between them. "Hey, Mr. Devlin, we're all starving. Can you order our pizzas now?" He shifted his attention to Cam. "Say, is it true what those stunt men said?"

"And just what did they say?" She surveyed his animated features and found herself smiling.

"That you were all in the monster movie we just saw and that you got killed three times."

"Three? Nope. I think it was four. Let's see—I was hit by a runaway bus, electrocuted by downed power lines, in a car crash, and vaporized by the monster's bad breath." Cam winked at Thor.

"Oh, wow!" Billy took possession of her hand and, plying her with one question after another, led her to the arcade corner.

Thor watched Cam mix easily and quickly with the teenagers. She was natural and didn't try to impress anyone. That in itself made a stronger impression. Her patience, wit, and spontaneous laugh proved an instant hit.

After he'd ordered the pizzas and drinks, Thor stayed on the sidelines observing. Cam played pinball and other video machines for fun, not for a competitive edge, yet, somehow she usually came out the winner. She was one of the boys; most of the time, better than the boys.

The excitement she created was contagious. Thor

found it impossible to continue being a spectator. But when he tried to play the electronic games, he was too focused on Cam to achieve any success. Little things about her stimulated his brain and triggered arousal.

To his blue eyes her animated features blushed enchantingly. He noticed a tiny gold bead piercing her lobe and his fingers itched to touch the silken blond hair that curled around the earring.

Thor's gaze followed the scooped neck on her sweater, the fine-textured white knit contouring her full breasts and teasingly delineating her nipples. As Cam stretched to retrieve a wayward bowling disk, he couldn't help but notice the smooth fit of her jeans across her rounded buttocks. When her leg brushed against his, he silently cursed the rough denim that shielded her smooth, sleek skin from him.

There was a unique relationship between Cam and the stunt men. A tender, devoted camaraderie that bothered Thor, perplexed him because he couldn't understand it, annoyed him because he wasn't part of it.

Passion ignited inside him for the happy, flushed woman standing beside him. A fever heated more than his body—it attacked his heart, mind, and soul. Thor needed to make something special, something unique, something infinite happen between the two of them.

But surrounding Thor were ten noisy pizza-munching, soda-drinking, game-playing teenage boys and five hulking, laughing, beer-swilling stunt men. Just the thought of trying to escape for five private quiet minutes with Cam was so utterly ludicrous that Thor found himself laughing!

"I wouldn't laugh at a bowling score that low," Cam teased. "Let's see if you're a better shooter than bowler. I'll get some more quarters and meet you at the O.K. Corral."

"Wait a sec, I've got change—"

Quickly, her hand moved to cover his shirt pocket. "We're going to need more than that!" She disappeared into the crowd before Thor had a chance to say another word.

With an acquiescent shrug, he wandered over to the laser rifle machine. He might as well try a practice round. As he delved into his shirt pocket crunching paper interfered with his capturing a quarter.

Thor opened the tiny folded square and read: *Five minutes, isn't that what you said? Turn left at the jukebox, then thru the first door on the right.* The name *Cam* was scrawled beside a cartoon face whose smile was nothing compared to Thor's.

Left at the jukebox. Thor walked down the dimly lit hallway. First door on the right. He squinted at the white paper affixed to the wood but it proved blank, not another note. Thor opened the door.

The room was dark, cool, and—his nose twitched—smelled of cherries. "Cam?" His whisper haunted among the moving shadows.

"You've entered where no man has gone before." A fluorescent column half shimmered to life. "Welcome to the ladies' room." Cam laughed. "You should see the horrified expression on your face!"

"I can, in the mirror behind you."

"Relax. This is the powder room portion, the facilities are another door away. There's a nice long padded bench," her hand smoothed the red velveteen, "and listen," she tilted her head, "there's also quiet. And since I'm the only lady in the restaurant, I think I can safely guarantee five minutes alone. Ah, your grimace turned into a grin."

"What a clever woman you are, Camilla Stirling."

Her lashes lowered demurely. "Compliments will get you everywhere."

"Now there's an invitation if I ever heard one!" Thor

moved quickly to sit beside her. His large hands cupped her face, his thumbs gently lifted her chin.

"And what are you looking for?"

"That cute dimple in your right cheek." His fingertip coaxed it out of hiding. "Ah, there it is." His lips pressed in a delicate kiss. "Have I told you yet how beautiful you are?"

"Now you have, but I'd love to hear it again."

He leaned closer, letting his forehead rest against hers. "You are very beautiful."

Her fingers played with the metal points on the collar of his light blue shirt. "Tell me more."

"I do have a confession to make."

"You sound and look serious." Cam gave his shirt lapels a tug. "Out with it, Mr. Devlin." She watched the corners of his eyes crinkle briefly before the lids lowered. "Can't be that bad."

"I'm embarrassed to admit . . ." He swallowed hard, sighed, then continued. "Ah, hell, I'm jealous!"

"Jealous? Jealous!" Her thumb and forefinger gripped his strong chin, forcing his gaze to meet hers. "What's causing this jealousy?"

"You."

"Me?"

"Maybe not you, not exactly." He rubbed his neck, his hand came away damp with sweat. "Damn, I wish I'd kept my big mouth shut."

"Well, you didn't and now's not the time to shut it. So explain away." Cam's head tilted engagingly. "Hmm, you know, I think I do see a little green right around here." Her fingernail followed the square curve of his jaw.

"Very funny." But he didn't pull away. "I know I shouldn't be feeling what I'm feeling but I can't help myself. Does that make sense?"

Cam nodded in the affirmative but said, "No. Just when did this feeling first occur?"

"When I watched that makeup man, Darrell Whatshisname—"

"Darrell Booth."

"Whatever! I didn't like—I couldn't stand—it made me so angry when I saw him touch you—" Thor's voice was a whisper. "I wanted to rip his fingers off."

Cam waited for his breathing to stabilize. "When Darrell or any other man slaps on the makeup it doesn't affect me in the least. It's all work. Nothing playful. Totally unstimulating. Rather sanitized and antiseptic.

"After all, there are touches." She patted his shoulder. "And touches." Her soft fingertips zigzagged a sinuous squiggle from his left temple across his large cheekbone to ruffle the thick brown hairs of his mustache. "Now why didn't that bring out a smile?"

"I suppose I might as well put my other foot in my mouth," Thor's lips quirked. "I—I was wondering about you and those stunt men. I mean, well, uh, you're all so, you know, affectionate."

"We've all worked together for over nine years on so many movie and TV projects that I guess we do project a *family* image. We horse around a lot, but that eases the nerves. And, yes, I suppose our affections for one another show. So does our trust, especially on the job where it counts." She ruffled his mustache again. "But to them, I'm like their little sister or just one of the boys."

"One of the boys?" His hands slid slowly up her bare arms. "You don't feel like one of the boys. You're soft and satiny." He pulled her onto his lap, tight against his chest. "And wonderfully lumpy."

"Oh, really?" Her fingers weaved amid the virile curls on his nape, pushing his head close. "I don't taste like one of the boys either."

Her tongue enticingly outlined his sensuous mouth, then teased apart his lips. A low groan escaped Thor. He took control, his mouth compelling and purposeful.

His kisses were erotic and full of excitement and promise. And Cam easily became lost in the sensations his mouth and hands were creating.

More than pleasure came from his touch. She knew no anxiety or uncertainty, just exhilarating feelings of rightness, completeness, and happiness that awakened every fiber of her being.

"Now you do the most delightful things to me," she whispered in Thor's ear. Her tongue made a flirty visit inside, her teeth playfully nipped at his lobe. "Jealousy all gone?"

His mustache brushed the sensitive pulse on her neck. "When I'm with you the strangest thing happens." He kissed the cleft in her chin. "Nothing and no one seems to exist. Just us. And that makes me so very happy. Does that sound silly?"

Her lips brushed against his cheekbone. "No, because the same thing happens to me. Seems we're suffering from the same disease."

"I have the perfect cure."

The glint in his eyes was both dangerous and thrilling. Cam wrapped her arms tightly around his neck. "What is your prescrip—"

A squeal alerted them that the rest room door was being opened. The petite waitress's dark eyes widened at the sight of them and she hastily backed out.

Cam sighed. "I forgot about Jennifer. I guess our five minutes are—"

Jennifer pushed in. "I'm sorry but—" Darting past, she went into the lavatory.

Thor looked at Cam and laughed. "Her expression was worse than mine!"

"We both should leave her a big tip." She slid off his

lap and straightened her clothes. "I'd better herd the guys into the Jeep. They've got a four A.M. makeup call tomorrow and I've got to dive off the waterfall. Now, what are you grinning about?"

He stretched his arms, his hands locking at her waist. "For the first time, my stomach didn't lurch when you mentioned jumping off the waterfall. Guess I'm getting used to your strange career."

Cam kissed the top of his head. "Or just trusting my talents more? Ouch!" She slapped at the masculine fingers that squeezed her waist.

"I'm properly chastised. And you're right. Again. I'd better exit before Jennifer comes out." He long-legged it to the door. "Say, any chance of you coming out to the ranch for dinner tomorrow night? We could finish playing doctor." Thor's wink was broad and leering.

"I think that could be arranged. Oh, here comes Jennifer. I'll be out around six?" She watched him nod and glide out the door in one swift motion.

Cam sat, just staring at her reflection in the vanity mirror for a good ten minutes. She wasn't quite sure what she was hoping to see. Her eyes did appear brighter, happier. Her complexion glowed without benefit of blusher. Even her hair seemed to have a sheen that wasn't there when she'd left her trailer.

Perhaps the biggest changes were the ones that couldn't be reflected in a mirror. Her heart and mind were in perfect harmony in their feelings for Thor Devlin. "No, no, not just feelings," Cam whispered. "Love. I love him." The face in the mirror smiled.

Thor watched through the restaurant's front window as Cam literally seat belted five slightly drunk, very sleepy stunt men into the Jeep and drove off.

"Nice surprise seein' the cat lady here," Nate stated. "The boys sure enjoyed talkin' to her. Reckon you did too."

106

"She's coming out to the ranch tomorrow." Thor fixed the red-checkered drapes. "I want something special for dinner."

Nate bit a plug of wintergreen tobacco and shifted it to his right cheek. "Gonna be a little odd, you two eatin' different from the rest of your company."

"Rest of what company?"

The foreman cackled. "Ya done it again, son. Plumb forgot about everything else but her. Tomorrow night's your turn for the Fresh Air Fund bar-bee-que. We got a good sixty people comin'." Nate elbowed Thor in the ribs. "But there's a lot better smoochin' places at the ranch than they got here!"

CHAPTER SIX

"You certainly know how to make an entrance!"

"Jack let me borrow the helicopter but I've got a curfew." Cam smiled into Thor's handsome face. "I see our quiet dinner for two has turned into," she peered over his shoulder, "um, dinner for sixty?"

"Try a barbecue for seventy-three adults and, well, I've lost count of all the kids."

"And to think it was only yesterday that you were desperate for five *private* minutes alone with me." Her forlorn expression didn't match her teasing voice. "How quickly the man's passion fades."

"Don't you believe it!" His whisper growled into her ear. "I actually forgot about all these people." Thor slid his arm around her. "That's the effect you have on me!"

He gave her a quick, hard squeeze and kept his hand possessively in the curve of her waist. "Every summer we have a fund-raising barbecue for the Fresh Air program, this year was my turn to play host. Good thing Nate was on top of all the plans or everyone would have gone hungry and thirsty and I would have been mighty embarrassed.

"As it is, I'm embarrassed anyway. I should have tried to contact you and explain what was going on but," his mustache quivered above a wide smile, "I wanted you here no matter what."

Cam turned toward Thor. Her fingertips flowed along the groove in his right cheek. "I'm very glad to be here no matter what."

With an eye toward the crowd that was just two dozen steps beyond the home pasture gate, she added, "Seems to be a rather well-dressed group."

"Anytime there's a party, we all like to show off."

Her lashes fluttered coquettishly. "Well, your hunter-green chamois shooting shirt hits my mark."

"You're blushing again, Miss Stirling!"

"Over my own plain attire, Mr. Devlin." Cam waved a greeting to Nate as the foreman busied himself with the lock on the fence rail. "Usually I can borrow from the wardrobe department but on this picture the clothing is truly prehistoric.

"So," she skipped three steps ahead of Thor, executed a graceful pirouette, then resumed walking by his side, "you get me in my newest jeans, my oldest moccasins, my brother's white shirt, and John Wayne's belt. Whoops!" Her hand stopped the swinging gate.

"Sorry, ma'am, but did you say you was wearin' the Duke's belt?"

"Wayne's one of Nate's heroes," Thor explained, securing the gatepost.

"My grandmother's too," Cam added. "In fact, it's really her belt." She unhooked the buckle and handed it to Nate. "John Wayne gave this to her in 1939 during the filming of *Stagecoach—*"

"*Stagecoach,* huh." Nate's eyes and fingers were caressing each of the twenty-five turquoise nuggets set in the sterling silver buckle. "That's my favorite movie."

"He trampled my grandmother with his horse twice, shot her three times—"

"Ah, the belt was a get well present," Thor joked. "And segueing from get well to well done . . ."

Cam sniffed the air. "Are we talking about your cooking prowess, Chef Devlin?"

"No, I'm talking about your waterfall dive."

"I didn't see you there!"

"Don't look so surprised. I was nicely tucked out of the way of all the activity and, using my binoculars, I closely tracked your climb up the path, watched you scamper over the rocks, and plunge into the falls." He tapped her nose. "On a scale of one to ten, your dive rated a fifteen."

"Well, thank you very much."

"I must admit I was glad to see you only had to dive once."

"That makes two of us, Thor. Oh, thanks, Nate."

"Thank you, ma'am." Nate's sigh was distinctly envious as he watched Cam hook the buckle into teak-brown-patinaed leather. Abruptly, he blinked twice and seemed to choke on his tobacco plug. "Say there, did I hear right? That the Duke trampled your grannie?"

Laughing, Cam thumped the brim of his straw Stetson. "Nate, my grannie has been trampled, shot at, and thrown off a stagecoach, train, or a horse by the likes of Roy Rogers, Hopalong Cassidy, Gene Autry, and, yup, Gary Cooper."

"Is she still kickin'?"

"She's a beautiful eighty-one years old and still as nimble as a teenager. In fact, she and my other grandmother have jobs on a new cops and robbers TV show."

"Well, I'll be . . . sounds like quite a woman."

"She sure is."

Thor stage whispered to Nate, "So's her granddaughter. And I think I'm going to show her off to everyone."

Cam was introduced to a close-knit albeit scattered ranch population. While names occasionally blurred into one another, faces and personalities were not only distinct but inspiring.

110

A dozen couples with young children laughingly labeled themselves "twentieth-century pioneers" and regaled Cam with hilarious misadventures that plagued their tenderfoot households. They'd all moved west for the same basic reason that drew settlers for more than two hundred years: the dream of a better world in which they and their families could live.

She discovered a majority of the ranchers were direct descendants of frontiersmen and prospectors who settled in Montana during the 1862 gold rush era or the 1865 cattle boom. Two families still owned private land parcels within the boundaries of the Glacier National Park that were held over from earlier days when hunting, trapping, and stock raising were permitted.

Cam felt relaxed, welcome, and decidedly at home. Here were people who didn't need social status or constant recognition. They worked together but at the same time were uniquely self-reliant, and the atmosphere they created was grown-up and reflective.

Thor held out his hand. "Ready for dinner, Cam?"

"I could eat a horse."

"How about an entire steer?" He led her to a yellow canopy that protected an abundant banquet. "Grab a plate and enjoy the feast. There's all types of salads, potatoes, corn on the cob, and a cauldron of the world's best chili."

"I see you weren't fooling about that steer," Cam added, taking note of the side of beef roasting over an open fire pit just outside of the canopy.

"We managed to get one before the rustlers."

She looked up from spooning potato salad on a sturdy paper plate. "Our chopper pilots haven't noticed anything unusual in the area where the movie company's been working."

"Seems the rustlers have moved northwest. They hit

Bill Peyton's place the day before yesterday, got three steers and a new breeder bull."

"Bill Peyton—wasn't he the one telling those funny gold-mining stories?"

Thor placed a thick slab of rare beef on his dish. "You pegged Bill all right. His great-grandfather and mine once worked with Buffalo Bill Cody's Wild West Show. Can I slice you some of this?"

"Half as thick, please." Leaning against the table, Cam watched Thor work. "There's some very beautiful, very eligible ladies around here, especially Bill's daughter, Irene. Why are you grinning like that, Thor Devlin?"

He cast her an amused, sidelong glance. "Because it's gratifying to hear that note of jealousy in your voice."

"I'm not jealous—"

"Liar!"

"I'm curious."

"About what?"

"Whom."

Thor exhaled an exaggerated sigh. "Why do I feel like I'm in an Abbott and Costello comedy routine?" He put the carving knife and fork on the wooden cutting board and faced Cam. "Okay, *whom* are you curious about?"

"Oh, you know, just general curiosity about your history."

"You're wondering if I slowly plodded my way through all the eligible ladies in Glacier country. Stop shredding that dinner roll."

She tossed the bread onto her tabled plate. "I'm feeling very uncomfortable and more than a little stupid for even starting this conversation."

"And I'm feeling very flattered." Thor's hands settled on her hips, his blue eyes staring into hers. "The answer to your question is that the U.S. Navy halted my slow,

112

plodding ways for four years. Of course, you know what they say about sailors." His wink was as broad as his grin.

"Girls in every port."

"Not *every* port. None were serious. None were ever left heartbroken. And none," his voice turned deep, husky, "ever made me feel the way you do and were ever kissed under a yellow canopy at a barbecue."

"You don't mind kissing me with all these people around?"

He checked left and right. "Seems we're all alone but even if we weren't," his head lowered, his lips moving against hers, "why, I'd kiss you right in front of your grannie."

"How about in front of Nate and Irene Peyton?" She whispered.

Thor gave Cam a quick, hard kiss, sighed, then turned around. "What can I help you two with?"

The foreman stuttered, stammered, and stumbled, but Irene smoothly came to the point. "There's a problem with some of the kids at the bunkhouse."

Nate nodded. "Buck's threats ain't workin', neither are mine."

Irene glided toward Thor. "Your threats always work."

"I'll have to remember that." He gave a resigned shrug before commenting, "Say, Irene, I've been wanting to ask why you're talking with a stiff jaw."

"Elocution lessons."

"You mean 'rain on the plain in Spain'?"

Her ringed hand pushed a sleek curve of ebony hair off her cheek. "Stop making fun of me and go play referee. Besides, I've been waiting to chat with Cam." Irene elbowed Thor aside. "We're practically neighbors."

Cam swallowed a mouthful of deviled egg. "We are?"

"You live a little north of Santa Barbara and work in Hollywood, well, I'm in L.A."

"Ah, Maurice Brennan."

"How did you know?"

Thor frowned. "Who in hell is Maurice Brennan?"

"Elocution teacher."

He blinked at their unison response and shared laughter. "Let's go, Nate, those rowdy kids are easier to understand and handle." He tapped his dinner plate. "Do me a favor and fill this up, will you, Cam? I'll be back soon."

Irene's liquid green eyes were watching Cam watch Thor as he left with Nate. "I apologize for the intrusion."

"No problem." Cam shifted her attention to the tall, lean, and undeniably elegant woman who was carefully making a selection off the vegetable platter. "How long have you been working with Maurice?"

"Six months. He says he can take the Montana twang out of me." Irene twirled a carrot stick into a rich, creamy clam dip. "How did you know it was Maurice?"

"I've worked with quite a few of the actresses he's trained. They all had a stiff-jaw quality when they first started. But he's very good. If you want that twang removed, stick with him." She began assembling Thor's dinner. "Are you headed for an acting career?"

"Public relations."

"Just starting?"

Irene shook her head. "Been an uphill climb for the last five years. Moving from copywriter to ad exec in the fast, frazzled world of advertising. Now I'm going to try PR. Maybe I'll be promoting an actress or actor you'll work with."

"What made you leave all this clean air for California's infamous smog?" Cam inquired, buttering two ears of sweet corn.

"It wasn't unrequited love." Irene giggled as the corn slid out of Cam's buttery fingers and rolled down the tablecloth. "I just wanted to relieve your mind. I know I'd be wondering."

"Touché, Miss Peyton. Mind passing a couple of napkins?"

"You should know, my parents encouraged a romance with Thor but neither of us were interested. Not that there's anything wrong with the man," she added hastily.

"I haven't found anything to complain about." Cam studied Irene for a long moment, alert to any guile or cunning but found none. "So, if it wasn't unrequited love—"

"Ah, but in a way it was. Love for that infamous smog, traffic jams, rock concerts, board meetings. I need to be surrounded by lots of people; I thrive on noise and confusion; I belong in a city, love its hectic beat.

"I've always preferred Ralph Lauren," her hand gestured down the front of her designer prairie outfit, "to unmarked, sturdy jeans. And Giorgio perfume beats the smell of hay any day!" She bit into a radish.

"Truthfully, all these wide open spaces, the quiet, the tranquillity, the aloneness—" Irene chewed reflectively, then grinned at Cam. "Frankly, my dear, it drives me bats. Mmm, I twanged just then, didn't I?"

"I won't tell Maurice. So, what do you do? Shuttle back and forth?"

"I manage a long weekend once a month. It soothes my folks' ruffled feathers. I stay long enough to annoy them and then, well, we're all glad to wave good-bye." Irene eyed her with interest. "You, though . . . hmm . . . I get the distinct impression you like it here."

"I do. It reminds me of home. And when you've been on location as long as I have with this picture, that's a calming, comforting thought."

"You must lead a fascinating life," Irene persisted. "Although you were quite modest when everyone was giving you the third degree."

Cam's smile was reflective. "I'd be lying if I said it wasn't fascinating. But believe it or not, most of the time it's just plain hard work. There's lots of planning, careful choreography, and well-timed illusions all merging together to make the impossible appear real."

"Ever date any actors?" Irene inquired, anticipation and delight registering on her fine patrician features.

"Now, I'd be very interested in hearing that answer," Thor's voice boomed. He laughed when both women jumped in surprise. "Well, Miss Stirling, have you ever dated any actors? Mind you, I'm not jealous." His expression was wicked. "Just curious about, um, you know, your history."

Cam's dark blue almond eyes were wide and innocent. "You're wondering if I slowly plodded my way through all the actors in Hollywood? Hmm, let's see." She held up her hands and slowly, without saying names, folded her fingers one after another to the accompaniment of Irene's giggles.

He growled, "Okay, okay, you made your point!"

"But I forgot to mention—"

Grabbing her hands, Thor let his fingers conquer and entwine with hers. He saw the laughter slowly fade from Cam's eyes, her pupils dilating into pools of black that shimmered with mystery and passion. He raised her hand to his lips and bestowed a kiss on her palm.

Irene cleared her throat. "I hate to interrupt. Again. But it's going to be tough to eat with your hands in that position and by the sounds of all the running feet headed in this direction, you'd both better look like your eatin' or those kids will razz you to death!" Her tongue clicked against the roof of her mouth. "Darn, I'm twanging again."

"But you twanged for a good cause," came Thor's resigned comment. He picked up two dinner plates. "Come on, Miss Stirling, I'll—Whoa!" He stepped quickly to one side as three teenage boys ran in and charged the food. "Let's head for more civilized surroundings, shall we, ladies?"

The main topic of conversation in the more civilized, adult surrounding proved to be centered on rustlers.

"Ever been bothered by rustlers on your California ranch, Miz Stirling?"

"Cam, please, Mr. Peyton," she smiled into his handsome, weathered face. "The only rustlers I've ever tangled with have been the movie kind."

"Did ya hang 'em?" Nate inquired.

"Two or three times a day," she returned matter-of-factly. "But you aren't planning to—"

"No, we're not," Thor added hastily. "Although we'll all admit the temptation's been great." A chorus of masculine affirmatives accompanied his admission. "This is just about the most efficient and elusive bunch of outlaws since, well, hell, since the Wild Bunch controlled this area during the first six years of this century."

Nate's face pushed over Thor's shoulder. "Butch Cassidy and the Sundance Kid were slick but they was caught. And we're gonna catch these varmints too."

"Here, here, Nate," Bill Peyton assented. "I'm wondering if these rustlers aren't part of an elaborate squeeze play. Remember all the trouble we had a few years back?"

Cam looked to Thor. "Squeeze play?"

"Yeah. We get a lot of oil, gas, or power companies wanting to buy up ranches for the land, which is rich in mineral areas. They pay a good price—"

"Too good," declared Nate.

Thor nodded. "And that raises the assessment value

117

of the neighboring land as well as the taxes. It takes its toll on the smaller ranches first but we'd all get hurt." He massaged his jaw.

"I don't believe these rustlers are in with any company, Bill. I do know they're sharp operators. Probably got a complete slaughterhouse on wheels in a tractor-trailer. What they steal and butcher in Montana on Monday, they sell for the same dollar value in Idaho on Tuesday.

"What puzzles me, though, is how lucky the rustlers have been." Thor regarded the thirty ranchers surrounding the picnic table. "We're using computers, freeze brands, varying our range routines, and checking the livestock at different times. Yet, they still manage to outfox us."

Bill Peyton thumped the leather holster pack clipped to his belt. "This handy talkie shortwave radio system you designed ought to do the trick, Thor."

"As long as everybody remembers to keep their radios in the monitor position," he warned. "The transmitter will break the squelch circuit and we can start our contact chain."

Cam listened attentively as Thor continued to answer questions about the new rustler-fighting radio network. No matter how repetitive or inconsequential, he deftly handled all inquiries. His voice and manner were calm; his responses were clear and concise.

Many of the younger ranchers were nervous and confused, but Cam had no doubt that Thor's relaxed authority gave everyone courage and confidence. By the end of the evening, the ranchers seemed assured that the rustlers would soon be roaming a prison yard rather than their ranges.

Citronella torches flamed to life as the inky night sky spilled across the waning purple sunset. The teenagers and younger children invaded the adult areas, demanding marshmallows for toasting and s'mores for assembling.

Conversations switched to a variety of lighter topics. More new and wild West sagebrush sagas were swapped, with Cam being pressed to talk about her television and movie experiences. She was enjoying the people, the ambience, and, most importantly, felt very welcome. Perhaps that had more to do with the masculine hand that tightly held onto hers throughout the evening.

With extreme reluctance, Cam announced that she had to leave. "The helicopter and I have a six A.M. call tomorrow!" With Thor's arm around her shoulders, she said her good nights. "I think Nate's farewell was focused directly on my belt," she said with a laugh as they slowly walked among the laconic shadows in the home pasture.

"My good-bye is going to be focused totally on you." He hugged her close, smiling when her arm slid around his waist. "You charmed everyone."

"They charmed me. And I," her head rested on his shoulder, her cheek pressing into the soft quilted comfort of the shirt's recoil pad, "I must admit I felt comfortably at home. You've got quite an extended family."

"That's a very perceptive remark."

"I'm a very perceptive woman."

"Oh, yeah." Thor swung her around. His hands moved across her collarbones and glided up her slender neck to frame a face that glowed ethereal in the moonlight. "And what is this perceptive, incredibly beautiful woman going to be busy doing so early in the morning?"

"Climbing the smaller one of your mountains. Seems someone recently erected a transmitting tower on the one I'd planned to scale." She laughed at his expression.

"Don't worry, it was a simple adjustment on my part and a minor soothing job on Jack."

His forehead rested on hers. "I totally forgot that you mentioned needing the mountains for the movie. The repeater that transmits the shortwave radio signals had to be installed on the highest point of land—"

Cam's finger stilled his lips. "No problem. Your smaller mountain is going to make my day much easier. Besides, the crumbling summit has eroded into buttresses and spires, making it look like a prehistoric cathedral. Even Jack was impressed when I pointed that feature out." Her smile faded and she went silent.

"Now, why is your very kissable mouth suddenly frowning?"

"I was just thinking about the safety of our movie animals with those rustlers on the prowl. Oh, you, stop laughing!"

"Sorry, I was just imagining the expression on the rustlers' faces if they ran into your animals in their time-warp disguises." Using the helicopter's cockpit bubble for a leaning post, Thor drew Cam close. "Now, what about the animals is troubling you?"

Her palms splayed across his soft, suede shirt front. "I was concerned about my horse."

"The black gelding imitating the unicorn?"

She nodded. "Zodiac is very friendly."

"I remember."

"And I've been letting him graze freely in your pastures. But those rustlers—"

"Keep the horse close," Thor advised. "There's no preference on what livestock they steal. Dick Sullivan's sheep have even been hit. I wouldn't want Zodiac turned into dog food." When she shivered, his arms provided immediate security. "Don't worry, last report had the rustlers nearly two hundred miles from here."

Adroitly, he tried to divert her attention. "So, you're

going to climb my mountain tomorrow. Did I tell you its name?"

"No."

"Kinnikinnik." His fingers combed through her long curls, the platinum strands a silken luxury that bathed his callused skin. "That's the Indian word for a plant that was substituted for tobacco when the real stuff wasn't available. You'll find an abundant supply on the lower trails."

"I like the wild berries that surround my campsite much better."

"You've set up a camp?"

"All the comforts of home, even a solar shower." She rubbed her cheek into the masculine shelter of his palm. "I just hope a mountain goat doesn't decide to eat it all. And why has *your* very kissable mouth turned wry?"

"It mirrors my confusion. That mountain trail takes less than an hour to top. Why would you need a campsite?"

"I'm not using the trail. I'm scaling the face, so I set up the camp just as a precaution and—" Cam blinked and stared down at her hand. "Your heart literally skipped a beat. I felt it."

"Kinnikinnik is five thousand feet high."

"A low, easy mountain."

"If you use the trail!" The steadying pressure of her hand on his chest made Thor take a deep, relaxing breath. "Those rocks crumble and crack in your hand like—like eggshells."

Cam's voice was calm and almost lyrical in its persuasive explanation. "I know. That's why, after my waterfall dive, Brad Owens and I spent the day in full climbing gear marking and checking every hand- and foothold and driving high quality, reliable, big wall pitons into the limestone. I even had the wardrobe department take my leather and nail-soled climbing boots and transform them into moccasins."

Her face went nose to nose with Thor's. "Your heart's resumed its normal beating pattern. And I think I can coax," her thumb and forefinger pressed into his cheeks, "yes, there it is, a very handsome pucker."

Cam placed a delicate, butterfly kiss on Thor's lips. "Hmm, now my heart's just skipped a beat." Her head tilted engagingly. "What do you suppose that means, Mr. Devlin?"

"It means, Miss Stirling, that you're very adept at refocusing my thoughts."

"Like you refocused mine off the rustlers?"

"Yes, but—" Another kiss effectively interrupted him. "You're taking unfair advantage."

"And I thought you had my work settled."

His forefinger sculpted the rounded curve of her cheekbone, down her jaw to center in the deep cleft on her chin. "I did. I mean, I do. It's just—"

Suddenly, Cam found herself wreathed by Thor's strong arms. She savored his lusty embrace for a long moment before becoming acutely aware that this man—this virile, powerful man—was trembling. Raising her head from his shoulder, she stared at him. "Thor, what is it?"

"I'm sorry." He shook his head sharply. "That didn't help."

"What's the matter?" She captured his chin and pulled his head down, bringing his eyes level with hers. "Tell me."

"I just had a horrible vision of you falling off the mountain."

"That won't happen."

"Two people would die."

"You're not making any sense!"

"Would it make sense if I told you that I loved you?

That when I'm not with you, I know what loneliness really is? And if something were to happen to you, I would cease to exist?"

For Cam, Thor's eloquent words were more potent, more forceful, more substantial than the sinewy strength of his body. "Would it help you to know that I've fallen in love with you? That I'm ultracareful, never leaving anything to chance because," her soft curves molded against him, "I have no intention of leaving you?"

"Oh, baby." Thor picked up Cam and whirled her round and round until he half collapsed in happy dizziness. "When did you fall in love with me?"

Cam laughed at the demanding note in his breathless voice. "Yesterday, at eight fifty-three, when you first discovered you were in the ladies' room." She tenderly stroked his cheek. "You had the cutest horrified expression on your face. And I could imagine that same expression—" she abruptly became silent.

"You could imagine—what?"

"No—nothing," came her stammered response.

His cheek rubbed against hers. "It certainly *is* something. I can feel the heat in your face."

She playfully slapped his shoulder. "Oh, you! If I hadn't stopped, it would have been all right, but now . . ." Cam reversed her position in his arms, her fingers fidgeting as they played with his.

Surprised by her tremulous voice and nervous actions, Thor decided not to press her any further. He rested his chin on her shoulder. "I fell in love with you a lot sooner, lady. You were constantly in my mind, overshadowing my every thought and I, like any normal man, was totally confused."

Thor smiled at Cam's giggle. "But all my confusion and my, um, well," he nuzzled the tender skin at the base of her earlobe, "let's be polite and call it—"

"Masculine reluctance?" She supplied, shivering with sensual delight at the erotic chills his mustache was arousing.

"Yeah, masculine reluctance. All of it, everything was unimportant compared to the love that kept growing inside of me."

The tone of Thor's voice changed. The light, teasing quality was dispelled by a sincerity and a commitment that made Cam turn and face him. "Heartbeat by heartbeat," she whispered, "the exact way my love grew for you."

Thor slid his arms around her, cradling her tight against his solid frame. "Oh, God, but I don't want to let you go. Ever. Stay with me. Here. Tonight. We've got a million things to talk over."

"I want to. Desperately. But," Cam pressed a delicate kiss against his lips, "we both have other people counting on us."

He groaned. "Yeah, I hear them. From the sounds of it, my neighbors are tuning up to sing every campfire song ever penned. You did it to me again, Miss Stirling," his hands cupped her face. "You made me forget about everything. We've got to talk. Really talk. Make plans. Damn! Is my timing ever off!"

"Oh, I don't know, Mr. Devlin, you caught me at the right time." Cam rested her head on his broad shoulder, her voice low and faltering. "Part of me wants to yelp for joy, and the rest of me is sadly geared to leave. And, Thor, I really must."

"Let me just say a quick good-bye."

CHAPTER SEVEN

A quick good-bye. Such a casual statement. And, granted, Thor had just kissed her. But the memory of that kiss thrilled Cam all night long and still provoked the most wanton sensations her body had ever experienced.

She felt her breasts swelling and when she looked down, the nipples had brazenly indented the costume's skimpy halter top. "Stop it!" Her forearm tried to rub away the tiny erections.

"It was only a kiss," she added in a haughty whisper to herself. "I have been kissed before." Her body's response made her groan and renew her warm-up stretches with a vengeance.

With her right foot hooked on the wardrobe trailer's outside exercise barre, Cam's hands grasped her ankle. She did a variety of flexes and stretches designed to strengthen the quadriceps and hamstring muscles. She'd hoped her willpower would also be fortified—it wasn't.

Thor's image prevailed over the noisy, bustling machine and peopled movie set and her own limbered, sweaty anatomy. "Oh, love, how I hated to leave you." Her hushed declaration curved her lips in a smile, a smile that turned smug and voluptuous as Cam dreamily remembered last night.

It was as if his kiss was the first haunting note of their

fully orchestrated love. Thor's mouth had been warm and firm and deliciously possessive. She had felt he was kissing not just her lips but her heart, her very soul. Cam couldn't help but focus on how absolutely wonderful it was to be alive and in love and a woman, especially knowing that her love was truly reciprocated.

Whenever she was with Thor, she felt secure, comfortable, and—her lashes lowered—terribly sexy. If his kisses caused such a reaction, she could just image what making love with him was going to be like.

Her heel slid from the barre, throwing Cam off-balance and onto the ground. Coughing and sneezing away a noseful of dust, she stood up, posturing in a t'ai chi meditation position and hoped a few minutes of slow, relaxed, circular movements would harmonize her yin-yang.

The continual popping and snapping of bubble gum broke into her cerebrations. Turning, Cam discovered Jack's watchful eyes studying her. "Are you ready?"

"Just about. We've got things to discuss." He turned the Pirates' baseball cap backward on his bald head. "By the way, that Japanese routine looks good on you. Jane Fonda know about it?"

"It's Chinese. T'ai chi ch'uan, and it means the grand, ultimate fist. Originally third-century boxing, now a form of kung fu martial arts self-defense."

"Self-defense, huh? Well, don't aim your fist at me when you hear my good news/bad news," he snapped the gum. "Two of the choppers are down, which means we're going to have to do triple duty with the small one and it's going to take longer to shoot." Jack frowned. "This is going to be a pain in the butt."

"Literally for me," came her dry rejoinder. "Why don't we wait?"

"Because the sky is perfect." His expression turned happy. "Sullen. Ancient. As rough and tumble as the

126

rocks. If I'm lucky I'll get some jagged lightning."
When he saw her left eyebrow arch, Jack hastily added,
"Far away from you, of course, kid. Your safety is my
main concern."

Cam reached down and tugged his bushy black
beard. "We agree on that. You haven't changed the
script again, I hope?"

"Nope. Not for the stampede or your climb. On paper, everything looks good and everyone's followed
your plans to the letter. You haven't failed me yet, Cam.
You've planned your moves right to the cameras, you
know where I want the slipping and the fending off of
the pterodactyl." He flipped through the pages on his
clipboard. "I am making a few changes with the animals. Where's the trainer and that tiger?"

"Pumpkin's staked out by the food trailer playing
with balloons. You'd swear he was a big kitten."

"Sure, that's because he doesn't growl at you. He
hates me. I said no to his last salary demand." Switch-
ing his hat around, he drew himself up to his full Napoleonic height. "But neither man nor beast intimidates
Jack Kenyon. Head on over to the set, Cam. I'll be right
there and we can get this show on the road."

Seconds later, the thunderous growls and roars that
interrupted Jack's high decibel voice had Cam and the
entire movie crew laughing.

Thor arrived early—just not early enough. He'd expected to find the movie set in its usual stages of noisy
madness, with cast and crew yelling and running in
methodical confusion. Instead, all was silent and controlled under Jack Kenyon's bullhorned "quiet,-on-the-
set" edict.

He was on the back side of a massive grouping of
lights and reflectors all aimed on the mountain. One
camera was moving slowly down a fifty-foot bed of rail-

127

road tracks; another elevated on a hydraulic lift; a third was strapped to the small helicopter that hovered to the left of a vertical megalith.

But lights, cameras, and movie making were of little interest to Thor. He wanted Cam Stirling. He needed to hold her, to kiss her, to wish her luck.

Thor also needed to show off his trust and confidence in her abilities and to prove to Cam that her stunt work was no longer a fearful issue on his part. In the half-dozen hours they'd been apart, he had really strived to develop a personal maturity about her career.

Yes, it was dangerous and certainly not a normal job. But she was careful, competent, and thorough. Something Cam had said, about accidents happening to anyone, had really been driven home this morning.

That was the reason Thor was late. His senior ranch hand, Buck Taylor, had been thrown from a horse he'd been riding for six years. All because a bumblebee had been trapped under a saddle blanket. A wry smile twisted Thor's lips—so much for his previous boast about how safe riding a horse was!

He'd even enjoy hearing her say "I told you so" except, no matter where Thor checked, Cam was not to be found. He was walking toward a sound technician when, quite literally, all hell broke loose.

The earth exploded. Missiles of dirt and gravel were blown skyward with a violent *boom!* that shook the ground. Thor's natural defense mechanisms grabbed hold. He dropped and rolled for the cover of a nearby rock formation.

Two seconds later, his brain remembered a very important detail: This was a Hollywood movie set. Nothing was real.

A very sheepish Thor stood up, brushed himself off, and gave an audible sigh of relief that absolutely no one seemed to notice his bizarre conduct. Seated on the boulder, his reflexes much calmer, Thor had a broad and clear view of what was really going on.

There was more than pyrotechnics. Headed toward him and the cameras was a stampede of Neanderthal men, their ranks punctured by split-second timed detonations that sent more than two dozen stunt men catapulting into space. Hot on the actors' heels was the oversized, shaggy pachyderm-cum-mastodon, lumbering and shaking the treed landscape, plus Zodiac in his flying unicorn costume with the saber-toothed tiger poised on his back.

Thor watched in amazement as men, dynamite, and animals worked in perfect orchestration. He found the black gelding completely fascinating. Zodiac's jumping, snorting, and rearing was cued to the explosions; and from a spectator's point of view, the horse's timing was impeccable and impressive. Thor immediately understood Cam's concern over Zodiac's safety from the rustlers.

The thunderous action continued for a good ten minutes, then with Jack Kenyon's barking, "Cut! Let's reverse," actors, animals, crew, technicians, cameras, and other equipment swiftly, with minimal noise, dispatched and regrouped.

The bullhorned cry "Action!" reverberated in Thor's ears as he watched the prehistoric troops charge the vertical face of the mountain to the accompaniment of further percussive blasts. The distance was great enough to require binoculars and, unfortunately, he'd left his at home.

After thirty minutes his rock chair became mighty uncomfortable and Thor was about to abandon it and the movie set with extreme reluctance. He was there to see Cam but she had yet to appear. For that matter, neither had anyone else since the cast and crew besieged the mountain.

"I guess I'll try later," Thor murmured to himself, stretching his sinewy frame off the boulder. "Time to get back to work."

A chiding note from his conscience reminded him that there was little work to get back to, unless he wanted another laundry detail. Nate had declared himself Cupid, redirecting all the chores to the ranch hands and the teenage boys so Thor could spend time with Cam.

Thor appreciated it—until moments like this when waiting around and doing nothing proved a more difficult task than good old-fashioned physical labor.

He investigated the skeletal remains of the unused movie equipment, careful not to disturb any item but always wondering what magic each performed. This environment was a foreign, joyless one, especially when Cam wasn't around.

His thoughts shifted happily to her and the portrait that formed was potent and vibrant. The feelings that engulfed Thor also matched the goofy, sappy expression on his face. He didn't mind, nor did he try to shake them off—frankly, they made him feel invincible. Instead, he allowed himself this time to wallow in the dreamy wonder of love, enjoying every cliché that popped into his head.

Irony short-circuited his daydreams. Thor reluctantly had to concede that all those published reports on men in love he'd once ridiculed were apparently quite accurate. Hell, he was living proof! He studied the dusty tips on his well-worn leather boots for a long moment, grinned, then thought, *To tell the truth, love feels damn good and I feel damn good! Lonely but—*

Thirty seconds later, his peaceful surroundings and thoughts were disrupted by a ragtag group of tired, dusty Neanderthal stunt men and a food/beverage trailer. Thor hung around, hoping Cam would eventually put in an appearance; she didn't. He began walking away when a heavy hand settled on his shoulder and a voice garbled something he couldn't understand.

Turning, Thor found himself staring into a ridged-browed, scruffy bearded face framed by dirty, shaggy hair. Blinking was his immediate response.

One hand was held up, while a set of oversized dentures were ejected into the other. "I'm Brad Owens. We met at the pizza parlor?"

"Oh, sure." His blue eyes squinted hard.

"Baked and painted foam latex on the face, a very itchy toupee, lots of glued body hair," Brad's fingers moved to the leather band at his waist, "plus this big, furry diaper that ain't wearin' too well." His limited rubber grin was infectious. "Let me get us some eats."

Thor gratefully accepted the small cardboard tray that held a steaming container of coffee, sugar, and creamer packets along with two wrapped sandwiches.

"Here ya' go." Brad tossed two thick mats on the ground. "Makes sitting a bit more comfortable." Noting Thor's curious expression as he opened a sandwich, he explained, "The BLTs are cut in thin ribbons for easier eating. Our facial appliances and makeup have to last through a seventeen-hour day." Brad carefully sipped his coffee from a narrow straw. "I bet you're looking for Cam."

"You bet right."

"Well, she just got finished kicking six of us off your mountain. I dropped, oh, around two hundred feet or so straight into an air bag."

Thor stared at Brad for a long moment, then shook his head. "You sound just like Cam. Describing the most death-defying action in the most casual of tones."

He thought about that statement, then nodded. "Well, to tell you the truth, it's real easy to be casual about this job whenever I'm lucky enough to be teamed with the Stirling family. When they set up a stunt it's as guaranteed safe as anything can be.

"I've been working with Cam for over eight years. And when I first heard a woman was in charge I almost quit. Five minutes later, I was ready to kiss her feet in respect."

Thor's eyebrow lifted. "What happened?"

"We had a director that treated us like dog meat and studio brass that could have run a concentration camp. But Cam knew how to handle them and their demand for stunts that were far too dangerous. They caved in and the movie made millions."

Brad neatly folded a ribboned sandwich into his mouth. "Cam really knows how to handle people. She can take all us guys down a peg or two when we start showing off. That's one thing stunt women seldom do— show off. Hell, I hate to admit it, but they're better men than we are. Macho is a pain in the butt!"

"When do you think Cam'll be finished today?"

"Two of our choppers were down this morning, so the camera shots are going to take three times as long. My guess, it's going to be an all-day affair." Brad stretched and stood up. "I've got to do some inserts with the second unit director. If you want, I can get you some binoculars from the prop man and you can watch Cam work."

Thor held out his hand and found it grasped by a very hairy one. "Thanks. I'd really appreciate it."

The binoculars proved to be super range finders left over from one of those commando movies. The magnification they afforded Thor was startling.

Despite the dim, natural light, Thor viewed Cam as a bright image that stuck to the angular boulders like a mountain goat. She moved fluidly, crab clawing in the fog over loose talus and up fractured rock.

He watched her slow, steady progress all morning.

When the crew returned for their lunch break, Thor figured Cam would be airlifted down to join them. Instead, she remained on the mountain, the helicopter dropping provisions to her while she rested on a horizontal slab.

Brad reappeared with a gourmet box lunch for Thor and explained that Cam's stunt was going perfectly, even though Jack was upset because the sun threatened to shine. The canopy of dark-bellied clouds that piled around the giant massif appeared, at least to Thor's eyes, to be a permanent, forbidding fixture.

By five o'clock, Cam had climbed the mountain a half-dozen times. She made it appear easy. And while Thor conceded her mastery of the technical skills, there could be no disputing the strenuous toll it was having on her body.

Yet the filming continued. So far, according to Thor's calculations, she had spent well over fifteen hours scaling the precipitous, centuries old rock face.

The sun finally splintered the cloudy canopy, toasting the mountain in pink rays. With it, however, came wind. Through the binocular's strong prisms Thor saw Cam, her hair whipping her face, battling and defeating this new element.

Another danger appeared. A hawk circled overhead, casting an enormous, elongated shadow over Cam and the sunlit gorge. An anxious Thor held his breath, then relaxed as the belligerent bird of prey uttered a piercing scream that echoed down the mountain before swiftly flying away.

Sunset arrived. Waves of lenticular purple clouds swirled across the sky, changing the morose atmosphere to regal radiance, and with it, came the end of the day's shoot.

Thor clocked everyone's return. Cameras and equipment came back. Technicians and directors came back.

Jack Kenyon came back. The helicopter came back. Cam did not.

Pandemonium reigned. Thor was caught in the midst of wild disorder, confusion, and noise. He was poked, pushed aside, ignored, and almost trampled. The conversations that buzzed in his ears were either loud and boisterous or whispered and gossipy.

Jack Kenyon's voice dominated all others. The man alternately shouted orders, yelled ideas, or screeched insults. No one paid much attention; all were busily packing up and even quicker to disperse.

For an instant, Thor thought about grabbing a bullhorn and yelling something obscene but common sense taunted that even an earthquake would fail to garner attention. Confused and concerned, he decided to find Brad, almost missing the stunt man who was no longer in his prehistoric garb. "Do you know where Cam is?"

Brad held up his hand while he finished counting some props. "They're all here, Tony!" He turned his attention to Thor. "Yeah. She's spending the night on the mountain."

"Why the hell is she doing that?"

"Hey, take it easy. Cam's fine. She radioed that the winds were too strong for the helicopter to pick her up safely and that she was too damn tired to climb down on her own."

A muscle moved ominously in Thor's cheek and his words came slow and deliberate. "So she's just going to be left up there? All night?"

"Sure. She's got supplies. No problem. Don't worry about her; we don't." Brad stepped around Thor's powerful frame. "Excuse me, man, but I've got to get these spears counted, packed, and loaded so I can get out of here. Take it easy. Nice talkin' to ya."

* * *

Don't worry about her. Don't worry about her. Don't worry about her. Thor shook his head hard. But that didn't still the words, or stop him from worrying.

He loved Cam. He was concerned about her health, her safety, her physical and emotional well-being. To say she had put in an exhausting day was the classic understatement. To leave her tired, hungry, and alone on that mountain all night with the capriciousness of the weather to further batter her would be, in Thor's book, a crime. It took a half second more of staring at the primeval crag for Thor to come to a decision.

He was going up there! By his calculations, using the regular hiking path, he'd be holding Cam in his arms before the sun finished setting. A happy smile curved his lips as Thor made his way to where Pegasus had been grazing all day.

Thor rode the stallion at full gallop back to the ranch. Once home, he stuffed his saddlebags with warm clothes, added hastily mated bread and ham sandwiches, fruit, filled one canteen with water, the other with brandy, grabbed up a flashlight and a bedroll.

Nate's gleeful support and cheers accompanied Thor as he tossed the supplies into the Jeep. "Don't worry, son, I'll handle things at this end. You get along and handle your end."

He ignored the broad wink that Nate delivered. "I've got the handie-talkie if you need to get in touch with me about the rustlers. That's why I'm taking the Jeep. I don't want to leave Pegasus loose in the pasture at night."

"Hell, boy, I ain't sure if rustlers make a good 'nuff interruption for a man's love life." The foreman reached in and twisted the ignition key. "Get goin', son. Time and the sun is a wastin'."

Twenty bone-jarring minutes after leaving the Jeep,

Thor crisscrossed the lower trail with quick, sturdy intent. Up, down, up, down—the paths reminded him of pleats. Their distances were short, his progress was swift, the elevation steadily increased and so did his breathing.

He was glad to note the number of spider webs on the trails. Webs meant no bears had lumbered through. For even though Thor had his gun, he really didn't relish doing battle with the large mammals. Or snakes either, came the uneasy addendum.

But natural hazards notwithstanding and even at his extended pace, Thor found it impossible not to enjoy the scenic rewards of the climb. Rocks as old as the earth itself picked up the red, pink, and purple reflections of the dying sun. The air was crisp, invigorating, and heady with the fragrant tobacco smell of Kinnikinnik.

Thor breathed deep and smiled. Here earth, air, fire, and water mixed with the mountains to form an alchemy of creation. He was a part of it, at home with Nature, one with the wilderness.

His smile broadened into a bold, slashing grin. By, God, he felt damn heroic. Like . . . like a knight of old on a quest. Thor's chuckle echoed among the shadows that traveled down the slope. His thoughts focused on the reward that waited less than two thousand feet away.

Cam would be surprised, pleased, and wonderfully alone. Alone. Just the two of them. Talk about perfect timing for a change! Thor stopped, took a refreshing mouthful of water, wiped the sweat off his face, and rested on a limestone boulder. He was a little out of mountain-climbing condition. He shifted the heavy double saddlebags from his right shoulder to his left and inhaled a half-dozen times until the stitch in his side relaxed.

When he started climbing again, Thor discovered the muscles in his legs had already tightened in the brief time he'd been resting. Poor Cam. He'd bet she was twisted in painful cramps. He should have brought a tube of sport cream and some aspirins. Well, he thought, the brandy should help and—ouch! His hand felt on fire. He hadn't realized how dark it had become until he tried to inspect his hand. Thor reached for the flashlight clipped on his belt, aimed the beam, and discovered six fire ants had decided to make his flesh their dinner.

Thor flicked the biting insects off, checked carefully for any more relatives, then poured some cool canteen water on his skin. The burning was still strong. Recalling one of Nate's home remedies for insect stings was a mud pack, Thor clawed some dirt into his sore palm and was just about to add water when Mother Nature lent a helping hand. She rained on him. Not a mist, or a light summer sprinkle, or even random dollops. This was a drenching, soaking sheet of water that slapped Thor in the face and left him gasping for air. Luckily, the deluge lasted only five minutes, five very long, very wet minutes.

He stood there, blinking in confusion and feeling very uncomfortable. With a heavy sigh, Thor shook the rain from his hair and face, squeezed his shirt, and sluiced the water out of his jeans. Luckily, his saddlebags and bedroll were waterproof. When he reached Cam, he could change into warm, dry clothes.

Cam! Oh, my God! All she had on was that stupid little costume. Thor hastily threw the saddlebags over his shoulder, aimed the flashlight, and started up the footpath. An image of her all wet and cold and shivering propelled him into a run.

At this height, there was little grass or dirt to absorb the rain. The terrain was rocky and rough. Limestone

137

boulders were smooth and wet; the leather soles on his boots were worn and slick.

Before he realized the danger, he lost his balance. Flailing for a handhold, Thor's grip slid across the rocks. He stumbled, skidded, and bumped his way two hundred feet down a mud chute. A pile of fragmented rocks broke his fall.

Thor rolled off the sharp debris onto his side and tried to swallow down the heart that seemed to beat so brutally in his throat. He wasn't sure how long he lay there. But it wasn't long enough to stop the hurt or heal his bruised pride.

Struggling into a sitting position, he switched on the flashlight to survey the damages. The flashlight refused to shine. Thor tapped it against his palm and tried again. Nothing. He hit it against his thigh. Still nothing. He slammed it on a rock. Heard the telltale crunch of glass. Now he knew for certain there would be nothing.

Something wet trickled down Thor's spine. Wincing, he reached around and determined it wasn't sweat or blood—the canteens were leaking. That was just great! He was already wet and muddy and he sure as hell didn't need sweet, sticky brandy to attract even more insects. The battered metal containers were hastily shucked off, the saddlebags were gingerly returned to his shoulder, and, with a groan, Thor stood up.

For a second, his knees buckled through the holes in his jeans. Thor quickly stabilized his balance, regained his poise, and, using the light in his watch, cautiously and slowly continued his trek.

What in hell had happened to the moon and to his stamina? He wiped a sore, filthy hand across his face, rested a moment, then continued the laborious climb. Thor concentrated ninety percent of his strength on moving. The rest was centered on Cam.

He pushed himself. Step after step. His efforts were

plodding but they were progressive, and Thor reached the summit.

First, he heard the singing. Next, the most delicious aroma tantalized his senses. Then, a brightly lit campsite came into view. Finally, Thor saw Cam.

The hairs on the back of her neck prickled in warning. Her senses went on immediate alert; her muscles tensed, ready for action. Of course, Cam reminded herself, it could just be the eerie whirring of the bats returning to their roosts. Or another little rabbitlike pika gathering more grass and herbs for his rocky den. Then again . . .

She didn't turn around but kept up her nonchalant pretense, humming *The Sound of Music* as she stirred powdered sour cream into her campfire stroganoff and mentally assembled her options. The hot pan would make a dandy weapon; so would its boiling contents and the butcher knife that rested just inches away from the propane gas stove.

Lifting the ladle to her mouth, Cam pretended to taste her dinner while listening for another telltale sound.

She heard it. Breathing. Not the panting of a hungry coyote or a wolf, or even the slobberings of a starving bear. This was heavy, labored breathing, accompanied by ponderous, slogging footsteps, footsteps that kept moving closer . . .

Her hand secured the knife.

And closer . . .

Cam tightened her stomach muscles, preparing to pivot into a roundhouse kick karate stance.

And even closer . . .

She turned and yelled, "Yiah!" Blinked. Swallowed. Blinked again, the knife tumbling to the ground. *My God, there really was a Sasquatch!* Cam's eyes narrowed as she studied the shadow-blackened giant that loomed a mere six feet away and, a second later, her lips curved in a knowing smile. "Those guttural curses sound vaguely familiar."

She eliminated the distance between them. "Hmm, and I believe my head rested on these broad shoulders just last night." Her fingers brushed the crusted dirt away from his face. "Ah, now, there's a handsome mouth I'm very definitely acquainted with."

Cam pressed her lips against his but an instant later found herself unceremoniously pushed away. "What's the problem, Mr. Devlin?"

"I am." Thor shuddered. "I'm disgusting. Filthy. Smelly. How could you possibly want to kiss me?"

"Frankly, I think you're cute." When she tapped his nose, dried mud crumbled off it. Cam hastily cloaked a laugh with a cough.

He stared at her. "Cute? You were going to chop me up in little pieces when you thought I was the Northwest's answer to the abominable snowman." Stepping around her, his booted foot kicked at the fallen butcher knife. "Cute! I came to rescue you and I get CUTE!"

Cam winced. "Rescue me?"

"Yeah. Rescue you. From the rain."

She watched his head bob up and down. "It didn't rain here."

"I can see that! Apparently it just rained on me."

"Well, the mountain weather is fickle. . . ." Her voice trailed off.

"Then, of course, I was worried about you being up here in the dark." He spread his hands. "But it's not dark."

"Portable generator."

"And I thought you'd be cold."

"Fleece jumpsuit."

"Uh huh . . . and hungry . . ." His gaze focused on the stove.

"It's just a little something I threw together."

"A gourmet something from the look and smell of it."

She watched him wander around the camp, checking out the tent, noting all the supplies, and wallowing in masculine self-pity. Cam wanted to say just the right thing except she didn't know what it was. So she kept quiet and waited. The sigh he finally issued seemed a heavy burden.

"Just tell me one thing. I was worried about you being up here. All alone. You *are* alone."

"I am alone. And very glad to see you. Can I have another kiss?"

Thor ignored the laughter in her eyes. "Not until I'm clean."

"How about a nice hot shower?"

He groaned. "You even have one of those?"

She nodded. "See that pine tree surrounded by all those bushes? That's my bathroom. Solar shower, chemical toilet, towels, and soap are on the minivanity. Just help yourself." Cam inspected his clothes. "I don't think anything can help your shirt and jeans—"

"I brought extras. They're in my saddlebags."

His stiff movements to where the saddlebags lay on the ground made her scurry ahead. "Here, let me. There's a first aid kit back there too." Cam handed him a heavy sweater and fresh jeans. "I'll finish dinner while you're cleaning up."

Thor's only comment was a grunt.

141

CHAPTER EIGHT

The shower was warm and soothing, the soap fragrant and cleansing, and the ointment and bandages anesthetic and healing. And, if the truth were told, Thor had to admit there was a funny side to his whole evening. So why wasn't he laughing?

He knew why. Shower, soap, and gauze pads had done their job at restoring and improving the outer physical man. But it was the inner man that still needed to be resuscitated. That mental acknowledgment made Thor all the angrier—at himself.

His mirror image displayed a petulant reflection that would only look good on a two-year-old. *She'll probably think I'm cute.* His sulky expression was transformed into a manly scowl.

"The hell with cute!" His growled last word was swallowed as he pulled over his head the charcoal ragg wool shooting sweater that he hadn't even bothered to unbutton. He combed his damp hair with his fingers, took a deep breath, nearly choking on masculine pride, then, reluctantly, went to join Cam.

When she viewed his stiff posture, aggressive swagger, and thin lips, her cheery greeting and welcoming smile died. He was still closed down.

Ah, men. Cam turned and stirred the stroganoff. She wondered how many millions of years it would take

142

before they realized their masculinity was not destroyed by weakness or emotions.

She cast a sidelong glance at the moody devil who had settled in her camp chair. Cam doubted humor or common sense would be able to wash away Thor's abundant supply of stereotypical macho attitudes.

Having dealt with a variety of male personalities, both at home and at work, she knew time was the perfect healer. If you gave a man time, he'd gradually relax, gain a clearer perspective, reconstruct his supposed loss of face, and become more responsive.

Time heals all wounds. A little food wouldn't hurt. "For either of us."

"Did you say something?"

Cam turned and held out two dishes. "Dinner is served."

"I brought some sandwiches and fruit." Thor stood up. "Where's my saddlebags?"

"Drying out next to your boots and holster. I'm afraid the food—" The expression on his face made her stop. "This isn't nearly as substantial but it is hot and tasty." She shoved the sturdy paper plate into his hands, then settled in the spare chair she'd been using for a footstool.

Don't eat, his subconscious ordered, *show her how tough you are. REAL men don't need food.* But the tantalizing aroma quickly piqued Thor's hunger as did the chunks of beef, mushrooms, zucchini, and onion clinging to wide noodles. His defenses caved. He even accepted seconds, along with a cup of hot cider.

Cam allowed herself a brief smile while she tidied up. Thor appeared more relaxed. The muscle in his cheek had stopped throbbing and the tense lines that framed his mouth were less pronounced. She thought about offering him a pair of socks for his bare feet, then decided against it.

143

She opted for a safer topic. "Seems we're being courted by a full moon. No need to keep the generator running." Cam turned it off. "Not much of a difference."

"I needed this half an hour ago on the trail when my flashlight broke."

His scowl returned but she pretended not to notice. "That bright reddish object in the eastern sky is Mars. It only comes this close to Earth every seventeen years."

"Where's the wind?"

"Pardon me?"

"The wind. The wind." Thor pressed his fingertips together in a steeple and stared at her through them. "That's the reason you told the helicopter not to pick you up, wasn't it?"

Cam took a deep breath. "When we'd finished for the day, the wind was blowing straight and hard out of the northwest. I felt the safety of the pilot was more important than my spending the night up here." Her eyebrow arched. "Now, the wind has all but disappeared. *You* know how fickle the mountain weather can be."

Watching as the muscle in his cheek began to twitch again, Cam sighed and rubbed her forehead. Apparently all her compassion and placating was not enough to rupture his sullen behavior. It was obvious to Cam that Thor needed prodding and Time needed a feminine ally.

"Well," Cam yawned, "oops, sorry." She yawned again, her lashes fluttering almost closed. "Um, suddenly I am soooo tired."

Thor watched as she stretched off the canvas chair. The fleece jumpsuit formed a powder-blue wave that rippled over her lush, womanly curves. Her hands moved up the back of her neck, fingers lifting her hair into a golden fan that framed her head before tumbling around soft, sleepy features.

Cam shivered. "Oh, it's getting cold. Can't wait to snuggle into the sleeping bag." Her lashes fluttered again. "Coming?"

He cleared his throat. "I brought a bedroll."

"It wasn't with your things."

"Damn, I must have lost it on the trail." Thor stood and squared his shoulders. "I'll just toss down on the ground by the fire."

"There is no fire. I used a stove. Besides, the bug spray won't keep the hungry Montana mosquitoes at bay much longer and at this altitude the temperature will go down into the low forties."

Cam slipped a determined hand into Thor's. "There's plenty of room for two in the tent. My brothers just used it on a fishing trip." She pulled him inside. "See, the air mattress will easily hold two and we can zip open the sleeping bag as a comforter."

For the next few minutes, Cam kept up a running documentary on the ultralight, tunnel-shaped tent while she literally pushed, pulled, and settled a ramrod straight Thor on the air mattress. She ached to laugh but decided to wait until her amusement was shared. "It had better be soon," came her muttered declaration under her breath.

"Did you say something?"

A sigh escaped her as she settled next to Thor. "Yes. I wondered how you liked our room with a view. The no-see-um ceiling allows star gazing without bug swatting."

Another masculine grunt assailed her ears. Her smile was hidden under the pretext of burrowing beneath the thick down quilt. Lifting his arm, she snuggled close to Thor. When his body stiffened, Cam hastily turned a bubble of laughter into a shivery "Brrr, it's getting cold fast."

"I'm quite comfortable." His tone was hollow, stilted, and sounded foreign even to his own ears. Lips tight, eyes staring at the sky, Thor focused on one thought: *What a jerk I am!*

"Well, I'm freezing." Her chin rested on the leather patch on his shoulder, her hand splayed across the front of his sweater. "But since you're not . . ." One after another, she unhooked the wooden buttons, pushing the thick wool aside "I'm sure you won't mind if I try a survival technique I learned in a James Bond movie."

Thor heard ten little pops, then felt her bare skin and soft, full breasts conform against his side.

"Shared bodily warmth, um, that's so much better." In the bright moonlight, Cam watched the muscle flinch in his cheek. But there was still no smile. Such a stubborn man!

Her long legs snaked around his, her toes lightly scratching the sensitive sole on his right foot. "Hmm, I don't know about you, but I'm getting hotter by the minute."

Delicate, feminine fingers wandered a teasing trail through the path of curly hair that matted his sinewy torso. Her fingernails made long, slow zigzags over his flat stomach, the zigzags becoming tighter and more precise as they edged closer to the waistband on his jeans.

Thor's breath quickened and his eyes blinked when he felt her fingernail click against his zipper. "If you're trying to get a rise out of me, forget it."

"Oh, really? Well, I'm getting a *rise* out of something, Mr. Devlin!"

And then she heard it—laughter—rumbling deep in his chest and escaping through a finally relaxed mouth. Cam ruffled his thick mustache. "At last! I must really love you, Thor Devlin, to put up with such sulky male behavior."

"I apologize." Thor pulled her completely on top of him. "I guess I lost more than my pride on the way up here."

"Who says you lost your pride?"

"Me."

"Don't twist your lips like that!" Her fingertips re-arranged a potentially surly angle into a smile. "Besides, you didn't lose anything, except maybe your funny bone."

Thor stilled her hand. "Are you kidding! Hell, even your grannie could have managed that easy trail better than I did."

"Did you come up here just to prove you could climb a mountain?"

"Hell, no!"

"Then why?"

"Because, well, I wanted to be with you. I just missed you this morning. Watched you all day." He smiled as her arms looped around his neck, liking the way her body seemed to melt into his. "Frankly, I was angry. No one in the movie company cared that you were stuck up here for the night."

"But you cared."

"Damn right! I love you."

"Loved me enough to climb that mountain. In the dark. And didn't turn back even when confronted by tremendous obstacles."

"Well, when you put it like that . . ." He averted his eyes.

Cam rubbed her nose against his. "Isn't that exactly what happened?"

"Yeah, guess it is." Thor winced. "I am a class-A, number-one jerk." He paused. "Why aren't you contra-dicting me?"

She laughed. "I was trying to come up with something a little bit more flattering."

"Gee, thanks."

"Actually, you're more stubborn than jerky. And I bet you were very spoiled as a child."

"I'm an only child."

"I rest my case." She stroked his cheek. "When I finally meet your parents, I'm going to tell your mother she didn't spank you enough."

Thor's arms tightened around Cam's waist. "I wish you could meet them. Unfortunately, they were killed in a plane crash."

"I'm sorry." Her head rested on his shoulder for a quiet, reflective moment. Then Cam adjusted her position to stare Thor straight in his blue eyes, her voice firm but light. "That doesn't alter the facts one tiny little bit, Devlin. You are still a stubborn, spoiled man. For some insane reason, I love you anyway."

"And I," his large hands cradled her face, "could spend a dozen lifetimes loving you."

Gently, Thor guided her head down until her lips fused with his. "Mmm, loving you, making love to you, with you . . ." his mustache brushed along the sensitive chord on her throat, "and that's what it truly is, Cam Stirling, love."

He tilted her chin so their eyes were level, his voice a husky tease. "Now, I may not be quite as skillful as 007 but we both are navy men and sailors are always equal to any challenge."

"Oh, and what's the challenge?"

"You."

"Me!" She blinked in confusion. "And what makes me such a challenge?"

"The fact that you can be very intimidating." His mouth spread in a lopsided smile. "You are invincible.

148

Afraid of nothing and no one. But for some strange reason, I love you that way."

Cam took a deep breath. "Well, you're wrong. I'm not invincible and I do know fear. Like right now. I'm very scared."

Thor's fingers filtered through her silken hair. "Of what?"

"You. Me. Love."

"Whoa . . ." He held her fast when she attempted to slide off him. "Maybe I'm not explaining things just right." Thor cleared his throat, then placed his left hand palm to palm against hers. "Cam, I didn't know what real love was until I met you. Together we will create a present and build a future. I want to marry you. To love you. To worship you. You are the last woman I will ever love."

In the bright moonlight, she examined every inch of Thor's face. His wide forehead, large cheekbones, strong chin, sensual mouth, and his eyes—all registered honesty, trust, and love. Cam's fears began to subside.

Her fingers entwined with his. "I've never loved a man the way I want to love you. Totally. Completely. Forever. You see, you are the *first* man I will ever make love to." When the silence stretched on, she sighed. "You're disappointed. You expected someone who knew all of Dr. Ruth's one hundred fifty positions."

"No, I am not disappointed," Thor stated. "I will admit to being stunned. Especially with your living and working in such a—"

"Fast, notorious community," she supplied. "Well, what can I say. You got stuck with the last virgin in Hollywood." Cam smiled when she heard Thor laugh. "I do mix and move in rather flagrant circles and I guess that's the main reason I never got involved.

"Between college and work, I've seen a lot, heard a lot, learned even more. I was interested in absolutes, not

149

sexual physical exercise and hollow words. 'I love you' rolls off tongues with the same sincerity as 'coffee to go'. I didn't want that.

"I do want what my parents have. A very stable, very monogamous marriage that has weathered good times and bad, tears and laughter, yelling and silence. That is real love. Real life. Real living.

"And then, too, with all the bad germs running around loose, a person learns to be protective. Careful. I needed to be very sure, very honest, very committed."

Her head rested on Thor's chest, his heart a comforting, steady beat in her ear. "I've never felt so sure, so committed, so absolute before. Until you. Until now." Cam inched up, her lips moving on his. "So, what about it, sailor, still anxious to break in a new but very willing recruit?" She squealed, her hands clamping protectively on his broad shoulders, as Thor tumbled her over on her back.

"So, Dr. Ruth says one hundred fifty positions." His eyebrows bobbed up and down suggestively. "Really? Hmm, the one hundred fiftieth one stumps me."

Cam giggled and snuggled closer. "Are you going to show me a few maneuvers?"

"You seem to know a few yourself—my clothes?"

Her lashes fluttered. "What can I say. I've read all the books, seen all the movies. Just never found anyone I wanted to practice on."

Thor's eyes glinted. "I'd be delighted to have you practice on me." His kiss was quick and hard. "Only me."

"In that case," her hands slid along his wool-covered shoulders, "I only managed to get you half out of your sweater and you're still wearing your jeans."

"Easily removed as is this fleecy thing you're still clutching."

Before Cam finished expelling a shy "oh," Thor had deftly disposed of their garments with masterful finesse.

"James Bond had the right idea in shared bodily warmth." His arms surrounded her. "God, you're beautiful." He stroked her shoulders, down her spine. "Your skin is silk. Soft. Smooth." His hands sculpted her lush curves, pressing her ever closer. Against him. Tighter. His heated flesh branded its masculine imprint.

Cam's legs slid intimately between Thor's. She reveled in the contrast of the masculine, hair-roughened limbs that purposefully anchored her thighs. "You feel tough and strong." Her palms mapped the rugged sinews on his sun-bronzed chest, her fingers tangled amid the thick forest of dark curls, seeking and tracing the hardness of his nipples. A colorful patch on his left bicep caught the moonlight and her eye. "Is that a— yes, it is! Thor Devlin, you've got a tattoo! Let me see whose name is on it." She pulled at his arm.

He groaned. "Just the navy's and an anchor. I regretted that thing halfway through the process."

"When and where," she demanded.

"One liberty night in Hong Kong—mmm, what are you doing?"

"Using my fingernail to write my name over the U.S. Navy's."

"That feels nice." Thor rested his forehead against hers. "Another message." The light teasing pattern her nails were creating on his back proved highly erotic. "I . . . love . . . you. . . ."

"I like hearing you say that." She pressed against the firm flesh on his back, her fingers moving down his spine to his taut buttocks. "I like touching you." Her fingertips skittered along his hipbone. "I can't seem to get close enough." Her teasing turned serious, intense, and she became acutely aware of his quaking muscles. "Make me a part of you."

The urgency in her voice matched the fever that had taken control of his senses. Thor's hungry mouth devoured her lips, his aggressive tongue penetrating into the sweet recess beyond. Cam found herself responding freely, matching his ardor. His kisses were intoxicating, her tongue became a willing mate in an intimate duel.

His hands blessed her skin with a seductive massage. As his callused fingers sculpted her breasts with slow, circular motions, she found her pleasure growing, overtly and without shame.

Cam kissed his ear, her tongue flirting inside before she planted tempting little love bites on his lobe. She played with the hair on his nape, Thor's brown curls sinuating their virile strength around her fingers.

Her breasts blossomed buds that pertly demanded attention and his mouth was delighted to comply. She arched closer, her entire body shivering with heat. His tongue washed each rosy peak, his lips gently sucking the sensitive nipples.

He lovingly pleasured every inch of her body. Her slow, sweet trembling heightened his own burgeoning arousal. His hand slid over her rounded stomach, a gentle finger delivered an exquisitely tender, but undeniably sensual, caress into the warm, moist center of her femininity.

Fire flowed in her veins, sparking every pore and igniting wanton, womanly desires that Cam never realized she possessed. "Thor, please . . ." Her voice was thick with passion, pleading for what only this man could give.

His face filled her eyes. "I want to please you, love. Just tell me what pleases you."

"You . . ." The word sounded more like a desperate cry. "Don't stop."

A husky, masculine laugh suddenly dissolved into a pleasurable moan deep within Thor's throat when her curious fingers fondled him intimately. "Do you know what you're doing to me?" His breathing was quick, heavy.

"Bringing you as much ecstasy as you bring to me."

"More. Your touch feels like satin. Wonderful. Much too wonderful." He nuzzled her neck, nipping her skin. "I'm afraid my self-control is just about gone."

Her arms tightened around his waist. "Mine disappeared the minute you kissed me."

"I love you." With that promise, Thor slowly, carefully fused with her. The erotic friction registered an emotional earthquake that encompassed more than two bodies—it united two hearts, two minds, two souls.

He remained perfectly still, savoring the wonder of their first intimate duet. Then he began to move. The awareness of him inside of her stimulated Cam. She uninhibitedly matched the rhythm of his arousal.

Shallow and tender, deep and slow, quick and forceful—she was supremely conscious that Thor was creating the sensations but they were uniquely her own to savor.

And those sensations carried her beyond reason and reality to a place where passion, intimacy, and commitment interweaved and became love. Cam was lost, yet found. Afraid, yet invincible. Here, yet so very far away.

When she heard Thor whisper her name over and over, she knew he too was joining her in the special world that only they could produce. She gripped the unyielding muscles of his shoulders, hoping his strength would invade her with the same wonderful passion as his body.

But no power in the universe was able to stop her from crossing an erotic frontier. She felt on fire, her skin shot full of tingling sensations, her inner self exploding into majestic relief.

Thor gathered her closer, his arms and hands tightening around her as his body detonated in violent passion. His heavy frame collapsed but when he tried to move, she held him fast.

"Don't—I need to have you remain a part of me. You complete me, Luthor Devlin." Cam's wide blue eyes lovingly gazed into his face, her fingertips softly sketching each handsome feature. "You have the longest lashes. It's really not fair."

"Shall I tell you what's really not fair?"

"What?"

His mustache brushed her flushed cheek. "That all these years I've kidded myself that I knew life, knew love, knew happiness." His tongue traced her half-parted lips. "But love and happiness just started. Right now. With you. My life has just begun."

Her hand slid between them to where they still made a most intimate connection. "Thank you."

"For what?"

"Loving me. Showing me what love really is." She peppered his chest with delicate kisses, then giggled when she felt him hardening. "I'm getting a very definite feeling that you're going to show me again."

"Well, we do have one hundred forty-nine more positions to try."

CHAPTER NINE

"Thor, your watch." Cam yawned. "The alarm is jingling." Hunting under the down comforter, she checked the masculine arm that weighed down her hip for the noisy timepiece. "Here, turn it off. Oops, it stopped."

He squinted at the luminous dial, then lifted his wrist to his ear. "Well, it wasn't my alarm. Check yours."

"I'm not wearing a watch." She balanced herself on her elbow, letting her full breasts tease the hard male nipples buried under the curly hair that covered his torso. "I'm not wearing nothin'."

"Are you sure?"

"Positive." Her dark blue eyes were wide, innocent. "Wanna check?"

His hand took full possession of her breast, reveling in the velvety skin that soothed his palm, while his thumb began coaxing the pink nipple from slumber. "Hmm, doesn't seem to be any clothing here."

Thor flung back the plaid sleeping bag, his lambent gaze devouring her sleek beauty that shimmered under dawn's silver rays. His fingers walked the valley between her flushed breasts, down her stomach, traced her navel, then skirted ever lower. "Why, you're right, Miss Stirling, I don't seem to be able to find a single stitch of clothing on your gorgeous curves."

"Told you." Cam wrapped her arms around his neck,

layering her lithe body along his sinewy physique. "Mmm, you have the most gorgeous hairy chest to snuggle." Her knuckles flowed along the curve of his jaw. "I even like your morning stubble. It makes prickles, sexy prickles, against my skin."

"Shall I grow a beard?" His fingers threaded amid her rich, platinum-gold curls.

"Nope. But don't ever shave off your mustache." Her eyelashes flirted provocatively. "That's your most erotic feature."

Thor's hands slid down the gentle curve of her spine to the small of her back. His palms sculpted the soft, firm swell of her buttocks, pressing her pelvis tightly against him. "You really think so?"

Cam's lips tilted engagingly as she felt his burgeoning passion. "It would be the first time, but I could be wrong."

The pleasurable, feminine sigh that echoed in Thor's ear thrilled his entire body and allowed his senses no rest. "I love waking up with you beside me and hearing my name on your lips."

He filled the cleft in her chin with kisses. "And do you know what your most erotic feature is?"

"What?" Her toes curled in response to the wonderfully sensual ache that tantalized the very center of her being.

"You remind me of Chinese food."

"Chinese food?"

Thor's laugh was deep, husky. "Oh, what a pout!" He hugged her close. "This is to inform one Cam Stirling that she has fallen madly in love with a Chinese gourmet."

She strained back to stare at him. "Was this a side effect from your Hong Kong tattoo?"

"Some," he grinned. "But it happened years before. My mother was always one to experiment and she lapsed into a Chinese phase. You should have seen the expression on Nate and the other ranch hands' faces when they were invited for dinner and found thirty covered dishes instead of the usual meat and potatoes."

Cam smiled. "I can imagine. Now, continue, Mr. Devlin," she tapped his nose, "and, I'm giving you fair warning, equating me with Chinese food had better end up being supremely complimentary."

"Don't worry," came his sly rejoinder. "At any rate, Chinese night was always a family affair. Both my father and I were assigned all the slicing and dicing. Frankly, I enjoyed it.

"While I was in the Far East, I did a little research, adding to my knowledge. And when I was on my own and struggling to adapt to structured business civilization, creating different Chinese meals made me feel closer to home."

A soft smile of remembrance curved his lips. "I could hear Dad teasing my mother, hear her yelling at us to stop fencing with the knives and to quit eating all the almonds."

"Sounds like fun."

"It was."

Cam gave him a gentle kiss, then teased pertly, "So, enlighten me about Chinese cooking, honorable Devlin-san."

"It is a very respected art. As a matter of fact, Confucius was not only a scholar but a gourmet. The Chinese feel that eating is truly one of the joys of life, that nourishment of the body leads to a longer and happier life. There's a carefully sought-after relationship between the ingredients that go into a meal. The unifying principle is harmony."

"I am very impressed," she acknowledged, "but I still don't see the correlation between Chinese food and me."

"Then you haven't been listening." His hands settled in a loving embrace on either side of her head. "You've brought harmony into my life. You balance my, um, stubborn, spoiled side," Thor flashed a brief grin, "with wit, wisdom, and love. When I make love to you, I feel nourished, replete, satisfied, and immensely happy. And the best part is, one hour later I want to do it again."

"Ah, sooo," she giggled. "Has it been an hour yet?"

His eyes glinted. "Even if it hasn't, I still want one from column A," Thor kissed her mouth, "two from column B," bending his head, he tasted the ripe peaks of her breasts, "and one from column C," his hand caressed down her stomach, moving ever lower until his fingers tangled in a triangle of curls.

"Mmm, I'm going to love being loved by a Chinese gourmet," Cam sighed before his mouth consumed her very breath. Her tongue and her body alluringly flirted with him.

And then a rude jangling interrupted.

"Thor, your alarm."

He groaned. "It is not my watch."

They both listened to the persistent noise.

"A bird?" Cam guessed.

"Doesn't sound natural."

She swallowed hard, her hand splaying against his chest. "Thor, you don't think it could be a bear."

"Bears growl or whuff."

"How about a tagged bear? Maybe its forestry tags are clanking together. God, your holster is out there."

He hugged her close. "Tags are pierced in ears. They don't hurt or make noise." He cocked his head and listened. "Hell, it certainly sounds man-made."

"Man-made, huh?" She squeaked. "Hikers! Maybe a whole group of boy scouts have trudged up your mountain by mistake."

"Then I will get my gun," came his firm statement.

"I'd better go take a look." Reluctantly, Thor broke his embrace and sat up. "Any idea what happened to my clothes?"

"Everything was flung around. Here, check under the sleeping bag." As Cam pulled the thick down comforter up, the clangorous jingling grew louder. "Oh, for heaven's sake, I know what that is—"

"What?"

"The electronic wizards in our special effects department rigged up a two-way radio-field phone gadget for me to use." Scrambling to the edge of the king-size air mattress, she tossed Thor his jeans and heavy sweater, pushed aside her fleece jumpsuit, a toiletries pouch, and extra clothes to reveal a stridulous khaki canvas sack. As soon as Cam flipped open the top and picked up the handset, the mysterious jingling stopped. "Yes?"

"It's Brad."

Her ear was shattered by his racking cough. "You didn't call me at the crack of dawn to tell me you're sick. And say, you shouldn't be calling me at all." The smile she aimed at Thor belied the determination in her voice. "It's my day off. All day. Like Greta Garbo, I, too, want to be alone. I refuse to work."

"Can I get a word in edgewise?" Brad garbled.

"Make it brief." When Thor wrapped his arms and the open sleeping bag around her, Cam leaned comfortably against him. "And fast. I'm not working."

"This is not about work. Exactly."

"What is it—exactly?" she returned impatiently.

"Oh, hell, Cam, I'm sorry. I screwed up last night."

"Brad, what are you talking about?"

"Zodiac. I forgot to bring him into the camp. He's—he's gone. I had him tethered to a tree, intended on bringing him in, and then one thing led to another. Oh, hell, we all got drunk last night. You weren't there to

159

control us. Oh, damn, I didn't mean to say that," his groan turned into another coughing spasm.

She took a deep, steadying breath. "Maybe he's out roaming."

"Cam, the rope was cut and there was blood. I'm afraid the—"

Thor felt her pliant body transform into hard muscle with one spoken word. "Rustlers. The damn rustlers got him!"

"It couldn't have been too long ago . . . the blood was . . ." Brad hesitated, "fresh and so are the tracks. Hank's going to take one of the choppers up and have a look-see."

"Tell him to make a wide sweep, then stop up here and pick us up," Cam ordered, reaching for her clothes.

"Us?"

Brad's meek query almost made her laugh. "Yes, six eyes are better than two. In fact, I'll have Devlin call his ranchers together. Tell me about the tracks."

"Two vehicles. Headed southeast. From the tire marks, one is definitely an eighteen-wheeler, the other a Jeep or a small truck." Brad sniffed and mumbled another apology.

"Sorry just doesn't cut it, Owens," Cam gritted, then slammed down the handset. She turned to Thor. "Your rustlers are headed southeast from our campsite at West Glacier with my horse in an eighteen-wheeler and a Jeep."

"Okay, take it easy. We'll get 'em." He gave her a quick, comforting hug with one arm as he buttoned his sweater with his free hand. "I'll get my handy talkie and launch a posse." Thor frowned. "Where did you put—"

"By your holster and boots," she panted, struggling to yank on underwear and jeans at the same time.

Looking over the shoulder as he exited the tent, Thor

160

had to smile at Cam's speedy, fireman dress efforts that were punctuated with dire threats to the rustlers. Five minutes later, he, too, was ranting and raving—at himself. The portable transmitter/receiver was dead, obviously smashed during his climb.

Thor took three deep, steadying breaths and examined his options. A communicator was needed. Maybe Cam's radio rig would do it. He pushed bare feet into damp leather boots, then walked back to the tent, buckling his holster and checking his gun. "The transmitter's busted. Can we use your radio to call Nate?"

"Mine only works from here to the movie set."

The peculiar monotone of her voice caused Thor to stop cleaning mud from the breech of his revolver and study Cam. She was sitting on the plaid sleeping bag half dressed—literally.

Her jeans were at her waist but unsnapped or zipped; one foot was sturdily housed in white leather athletic shoes, the other foot still bare; her left arm and shoulder was cloaked by a blue and black rugby shirt that flapped uselessly against her naked right side.

"Cam, honey . . ." Quickly, Thor was at her side; his large hands framed her face, his eyes examining her despondent features. "What—"

"You're going to think I'm silly."

When she attempted to pull free, his arms surrounded her shoulders, holding her fast. "Never. Tell me."

"I feel as if someone has stolen my child." The anguish in her voice registered in her moist blue eyes. "I know Zodiac's a horse. An animal. But I raised him. Trained him. Cared for him. Breathed life into him."

Her hand closed over Thor's. "I was home alone the night the mare gave birth. It was long, difficult, and she needed help. The foal was malpositioned, the mare's uterus ruptured, and I dislocated my shoulder pulling

161

out the colt. His tongue was blue and I had to give him mouth-to-nostril resuscitation to start him breathing.

"The mare didn't make it, so I became Zodiac's surrogate mother. I moved into the stables, bottle nursed him, kept him warm, dry, protected." Cam sniffed, her lips curving in a soft smile. "He acted like a puppy and was treated like a baby. And now . . ."

"Hey, calm down, honey," Thor hugged her close, "don't let your imagination run wild."

"Brad said there was blood."

"No guarantee it was Zodiac's."

"Well, I just assumed. I never thought, but—yeah. Yeah!" Her posture and tone grew stronger, more forceful. "Zodiac has a temper and forty strong teeth and quite a kick. Especially since he's wearing cleated horse shoes. I hope he used both. I hope he tried to trample those bums. I'd like to trample them!"

Thor hastily scrambled out of Cam's way as she turned into a whirling mass of arms and legs that finished dressing in seconds. Cocking her head, she announced, "Chopper's coming, Thor."

Hastily, her fingers locked around a hairbrush. "I think you'll be able to use the chopper radio to contact Nate. Of course, Hank will know for sure. Maybe the two of you can jerry-rig something—"

The brush paused midair. Cam whirled to face him. "God, Thor, I just remembered what you said about your parents and an air crash. Do you mind flying?"

"I prefer ground transportation," his tone was wry, his grin decidedly lopsided. "But don't worry, I've been on at least a dozen planes during the last five years and haven't disgraced myself yet."

He scooped up the broken transmitter with one hand and grabbed Cam's hand in his other. "We better get out of this tent. The wind from the chopper rotors are buckling the sides."

Cam was surprised to see Hank piloting the large turbocopter. Once she and Thor were settled in the cockpit, headsets in place, she said so.

"This baby was the only one working," Hank informed her, nodding to Thor. "Good thing you waved me off last night. I just managed to limp back with the little one and put her down for repairs."

"Winds were too strong besides." She gave him a wink. "Us pilots have to stick together. I know how lousy Kenyon's repair budget is."

"You would have loved hearing Bridget ream him out last night," the pilot grinned. "She's had it with this cafeteria for wildlife. Some marmots got into her gourmet dinner last night—before she did."

"Must have been a fun evening."

"I stayed in my trailer and watched the Disney channel." Hank popped his chewing gum. "Okay, baby, shall I tell you what I didn't find?"

"The rustlers."

"Right. With this chopper, I made an easy forty-mile southeast sweep in the last half hour." He handed Cam a marked area map. "Nothing. Not even dust."

"That's damn rugged country in that area," Thor remarked. "Trying to navigate a tractor-trailer would be time-consuming and tricky." He studied the map for a moment. "Hmm, I wonder. What if they weren't finished for the day but just starting? Then they'd head south and west looking for far pasture steers, sheep, equipment."

Thor tapped the copter's radio mike. "Can we make a telephone patch?" At Hank's nod, he grinned at Cam. "I'll call Nate and he can mobilize in that direction."

Her hand stalled his. "We can get there quicker." Cam's eyes locked into his. "Are you game?"

"Let's go."

"Okay, Henry, show Devlin what makes you the best chopper pilot in the business."

Despite its size, the jetcopter was smooth, agile, and fast. In fifteen minutes, they'd covered more than thirty air miles and, with an extra boost from high-powered, rangefinder binoculars, they had a clear field of vision for nearly twenty miles in every direction.

"Try a more northerly heading," Thor instructed Hank, pointing to the map. "The terrain is easier but still sheltered by mountain shadows."

Cam shifted impatiently. "Maybe they did go southeast, then north to Alberta." She grabbed the map. "Maybe you should call Nate and have him head that way. Or how about calling the state police? The Mounties? Or maybe they caught Route 2 and are heading for Idaho? Or—"

"Take it easy, sweetie," Hank cautioned, "all your jumping around is making me airsick."

"Sorry." She lapsed into a morose inspection of the landscape. Her eyes easily dismissed Nature's beauty as they intently surveyed the area for anything abnormal.

But as time passed and nothing was sighted, Cam's anxiety and fear multiplied until she heard Thor's "mmm" reverberating in her headphones. "Was that a positive or a negative?" came her nervous yelp.

"I'm not sure." He lowered his binoculars and gave Hank new coordinates. "Something caught the sun."

"Like a windshield? Or a truck? Or a Jeep?"

"Cam," he squeezed her knee, "it could be garbage. Let's wait and see."

"It's them!" She jumped excitedly. "I mean is that an eighteen-wheeler with a Jeep advance team or what?"

"Could be and then again—"

"Thor!" She handed him a microphone, her index finger tapping the broadcast switch. "You've been deputized by the police. Order them to pull over. If we're wrong, no harm done and I'll make all the apologies."

Hank pushed the collective pitch stick downward, then set the blades on medium to hover above the white cab on the slow-moving truck.

Just as Thor was about to transmit his order, a rifle barrel made an appearance through the open skylight of the cab. Hank's sharp eye and sharper reflexes had the chopper moving sideways, back, and up out of target range.

Thor's expression was grim. "I don't think we're going to be issuing any apologies. Let's put in a call for help."

"That's going to take forever," Cam muttered. She yanked out her communication/headphone jack and disappeared into the cargo hold of the chopper while Thor and Hank were busy relaying their exact positions.

She returned a few minutes later to plug herself back into their conversation. "When will the posse arrive?"

"Even with the repeater network, it'll be a good forty minutes. The state police copter might make it in thirty," he relayed. "I guess all we can do is tag them from a bullet-safe distance and make sure they don't pull their usual disappearing act." Thor formed two fists. "I wish we could stop them. Now. Right now."

Cam's fingers curved lovingly over his hands. "We are two people of a single mind, Thor Devlin." She smiled as a pair of puzzled blue eyes stared at her. "I don't suppose you ever saw a campy B-movie called *Pedal to the Metal?*"

"I—I beg your pardon?" Thor asked, totally confused as Hank's chuckle echoed in his ears through the headphones.

"You are in the company of two of its major stars," the pilot revealed.

"Three," she interjected. "You forgot the chopper."

"I still don't—"

"The movie had this same scenario," Hank explained. "One chopper full of good guys in pursuit of a truck full of bad guys with the cavalry too far behind to help."

"And this nice chopper is filled with all sorts of special effects goodies," Cam announced. "We've got a box of assault grenades, colored smoke bombs, ropes—"

"They've got a gun," Thor pointed out.

She patted his hip. "So do we."

He did some mental arithmetic. "There's four in the Jeep, two in the truck cab, we don't know how many in back."

"We've got a few things that can change the odds."

Thor flexed his shoulder muscles. "All right. Let's give it a shot. Hank and I should be able to handle—"

"Whoa, buddy!" Hank snapped. "If you haven't noticed, let me introduce myself. Henry J. Marsh, a bald, slightly pudgy, sixty-two-year-old father of seven, grandfather of five, and the proud owner of two ex-wives."

"Translated, that means he's a lover, not a fighter," Cam announced.

"Absolutely," the pilot heartily confirmed. "I don't even fight alimony. If you want a fighter, Cam is your man," his thumb jerked at her. "She's done four Chuck Norris karate films, three paramilitary commando movies, and hundreds of TV cop shows."

"And fought my way through a sale on Rodeo Drive." She dropped a box stenciled GRENADES onto Thor's lap. "Ever jump out of a helicopter, sailor?"

Thor's gaze shifted from the small, filled cardboard box on his knees to the woman crouched next to him. Confidence, excitement, and a dare-the-devil spirit radiated in her blue eyes and on her face.

Her attitude and mindset proved contagious and effectively vanquished all his concerns and doubts. Thor knew that the woman who'd be fighting alongside of him could do what he could do—half the battle was already won.

"Never jumped out of a chopper, just off the side of a ship," came his relaxed answer. "Sixty-five feet down into the ocean along with three thousand other sailors for a swim call."

"There ya' go," Cam winked. "But Hank'll get us closer to the ground than that. Say, four feet?"

The pilot grinned and nodded. "Same script as the movie, Cam?"

"Should work like a charm." She resettled into the cockpit seat to brief Thor. "Hank's going to fly high and ahead of their convoy. Then he'll turn the chopper around and come straight at them. The grenades will be our initial offering.

"Just pull the pin and bombs away!" Her amusement was quickly tempered. "They make a lot of noise and throw a lot of dirt but they're not explosives. Just a powerful surprise punch."

"But your rustlers won't know that," Hank added. "The grenades will shake them up, toss them around, and stop their engines." He increased the helicopter's drive, speed, and altitude after Cam went back into the cargo area. "After you two drop the grenades, I'll make a sharp turn and come at them from the rear. Low. That's when you release the colored smoke bombs."

Returning with another carton, Cam patched her communications plug into the console. "All you do is light this fuse and drop it—fast. And I mean fast! The smoke is a real irritant. We'll need to wear these face masks. Remember, breathe only through your nose. There's a special filter in here that will purify your air."

She handed Thor protective plastic shields fitted with side eye guards and an adjustable headstrap.

Thor's smile was twisted. "So this is your equalizer. Not bad, sweetheart." His fingers reached up to tweak her cheek. "Brains and beauty."

"The man says the sweetest things!" Cam fluttered her lashes. "Our goal is to aim these darlings into the open Jeep and hopefully drop one in the truck cab's open skylight." She reached over and unplugged Hank's headphones. "That's Dr. Ruth's one hundred fiftieth maneuver, Devlin, getting cylindrical objects into small openings from a high altitude."

"You're blushing again, Miss Stirling."

"So are you!" Cam reset Hank's patch, then continued in a very prim voice. "After the smoke bombs are launched, Hank will let us off, hover, toss more bombs, and herd back any escapees."

"Once we land?"

"Confiscate their guns and then do what comes naturally." Cam smiled as Thor's right fist slammed into his left palm. "Say, I hope somebody's got a match for these smoke bombs!"

Hank patted down his pockets and came up with a disposable lighter. "Let's run through everything one more time."

"You do it," Cam told the pilot. "I've got to fix up your smoke bombs and do a little rearranging in the cargo area for our quick exit."

She returned in less than three minutes, a shoebox in her left hand while her right was busy lacing ropes through the belt loops of her jeans. "All set?" Two affirmative nods were her answer. "Okay, Thor, come on back and I'll position you."

Hank waited until Devlin had removed his headphones to speak. "Cam, think he'll be all right? You're used to this, you do it every day. If Devlin freezes on you—"

"I've no doubts about him." She patted the pilot's arm, then reached around, placing a shoebox on the floor by the cockpit door. "Listen, I put some grenades in but don't drop too many extra smoke bombs. Makes for poor visibility."

"Gotcha. Hey, kiddo, just remember this cruncher's for real. Make sure your punches land on target, not two feet in front like your stunt fights."

"Believe me, they're going to land on target. Those damn rustlers picked the wrong woman to steal from. I just hope, for their sake, my Zodiac's still in one piece." Cam's expression was grim when she gave Hank a thumbs-up signal, removed her headphones, and went to join Thor.

Sitting on her heels beside him, she spoke right into his ear. "When I slide this door open, don't look down. Just keep dropping grenades. When Hank decreases power and altitude so we can aim the smoke bombs, then focus. The height won't be so dizzying." Cam heard the change in the rotors and felt the shift in pitch. "Don't forget to bend your knees when we jump."

Thor ached to say something fierce and commanding but her shout of "here we go" coupled by the sudden blast of wind from the open cargo door rendered him speechless. And when he blinked into view the spiraling aerial height, his entire body froze.

It was the swift, forceful movements of Cam's arm against his that brought Thor out of his temporary stupor. He grabbed two fistfuls of grenades, popped their collective pins, and, taking care to avert his eyes, heaved them out of the chopper.

Hank's sharp, banking turn sent Thor flailing backward. He scrambled to regain his balance, feeling chagrined because Cam had not lost hers. In fact, she was flaming the butane lighter into operation.

Thor followed her example on lighting the smoke bomb fuses, tossing three at random. Then, after taking a deep, calming breath, he scrutinized the rustlers' convoy.

The grenades had stalled both vehicles. One smoke bomb hit its mark and a dense, blue mushroom cloud belched from the open Jeep. Now, the helicopter was almost directly above the truck cab. Thor waited a heartbeat, lit a fuse, and dispatched another bomb. It missed.

He yanked one from Cam's hand and tried again. "Success!" A jubilant Thor went to hug her but discovered a lit, spitting fuse blocking the way. He watched her throw the bomb, then, without warning, her hand splayed across his face.

His eyes and nose were smothered by plastic. For an instant, Thor struggled to breathe. There was a shout, pressure on his forearm, then Thor's world shifted into slow motion.

He spent an agonizing, confused interval in the helpless freedom of space. The abrupt, jarring force of his boots slamming into the earth restored his sanity.

Thor staggered off-balance. Quickly, two steadying hands helped stabilize his weight and equilibrium. His blinking eyes registered Cam Stirling as their owner.

When he attempted to speak, her fingers clamped his lips shut. She pointed to the billows of blue smoke rippling in their direction. Thor tapped the nose filter on his face mask, acknowledging his error.

Her blown kiss was the last thing he saw as Cam turned and ran pell-mell into the colored cloud. Grimacing at his own lack of initiative, Thor swiftly followed suit.

Thor felt as though he'd been swaddled in blue cotton

batting. Pushing the thick, vaporous walls aside, he headed in the direction of all the shouting, gasping, and coughing.

The truck cab loomed, its door open. On the wide running board, a man was doubled over, gagging for air. Thor spied a rifle in the dirt and kicked it well under the truck. He grasped the man's shirt, hauling him upright, then landed a solid punch to his jaw. The weepy-eyed rustler shimmied to the ground.

Smiling, he checked inside the cab, anxious to find someone else to hit. But it was empty. Thor's senses were alert, alive, invigorated. He moved cautiously, his posture and stance that of a boxer. Grunting sounds assailed his ears. He angled toward them. Wary. Watchful. Poised for action.

All at once, his visibility improved, courtesy of helicopter-made winds. As the opaque cloud fragmented, Thor viewed a most astonishing sight. Three of the rustlers were facedown, bound wrist to ankle, broken rifle parts scattered around them in the gravel.

His peripheral vision was flagged by colors in motion. Turning, Thor recognized Cam. She was caught between two of the rustlers. But in the seconds it took for his brain to move his foot, he viewed her easy defeat of one opponent and her attack on the other.

Thor was mesmerized. Cam's movements were graceful, swift, and formidable. *Deadly.* That word registered a mighty blow in his mind the instant her foot connected a debilitating kick to the rustler's groin. She didn't stop there. The knuckles of her first two fingers aimed punches to his face until he crumbled.

Thor watched Cam pivot, her elbow slamming into her other assailant's chest, then the edge of her hand dealt a series of knife-stabbing blows to his shoulder, driving him down in pain. She then proceeded to pull ropes from the waistband of her jeans and truss these men in the same turkeylike position as the others.

He was trying hard to comprehend this—Wonder Woman—this female Rambo—when Thor found himself grabbed from behind, spun around, and punched in the mouth. His head reeled back but his left fist jabbed forward, striking the attacker in the stomach. He followed up with a right uppercut to the man's jaw. The rustler fell facedown in the dirt, out cold.

The taste of blood and dirt in his mouth only heightened Thor's masculine satisfaction. But his elation proved short-lived when he realized this was the same rustler he'd knocked out before! "Damn you," he kicked the thief's leg, "stay down this time."

An increase in walloping rotors made Thor look skyward. The state police helicopter had joined Hank, and both pilots were decreasing power and landing.

"The cavalry has arrived!" Cam shouted, running to Thor's side and waving to the descending copters. She wiped the plastic mask from her face and stared down at the unconscious rustler. "He makes six. Anybody else?"

"I think *you* got 'em all," came his clipped rejoinder. "What was that you were doing? Karate?"

She shook her head. "A mix of kung fu and t'ai chi." Cam flashed a grin. "Goes right along with your Chinese cooking and—say, Thor, you're bleeding!" Her fingers moved to his mouth. "Does it hurt?"

"I'm fine."

"And your jeans are ripped, your sweater's torn."

"They can be fixed." As his eyes shifted from himself to her, Thor realized Cam was immaculate. *Okay, maybe there was a hair out of place,* he rationalized, *but no blood, no dirt, not even sweat. She could pose for* Vogue! A muscle in his cheek twitched.

Cam grabbed his hand. "Let's check the truck. I just

hope Zodiac's in one piece." She eyed the trailer's massive rear doors. "Think there's anyone inside?"

Thor drew his revolver. "Part of me hopes so." He mounted the two metal steps, inspected the lock, then, with an order of "stand clear," he shot it open.

Neighing, snorting, and the solid sound of metal horseshoes kicking steel siding brought a smile to Cam's lips: "My horse is definitely in one piece," she laughed, anxiously waiting as Thor flung open the wide doors and pulled the interior loading ramp in place.

Thor grimaced at the immediate sight of three steer carcasses. "Our rustlers were busy boys this morning." Skirting the slaughtered animals, he walked inside, streaks of sunlight illuminating the dark interior. "More farm equipment and sheep."

He moved quickly, trying not to gag at the smell. The horse was at the head of the trailer. Thor fumbled with the knots on the reins, while voicing a soothing recital to calm the bucking Zodiac. Finally, the horse was free; both man and animal hurriedly bolted for the exit.

The black gelding clamored down the metal ramp. Nostrils flaring, ears twitching, he reared, pawing the air, then turned quite docile at the sound of a familiar voice. "Come here, sweetie," Cam crooned. "Did those bad men hurt you." She checked his glistening ebony coat for cuts and his strong body for bruises.

"He okay?" Thor inquired.

"Fine." She hugged Zodiac's neck and was rewarded with a lick and nuzzle to her own. "I'm really sorry about the rustlers getting more steers. Can you tell who was hit?"

"No, but the farm machinery should be marked." He looked over her shoulder. "Here comes Hank and the police now—"

"And here's Nate with the rest of the posse." Her

elbow jabbed him lightly in the ribs. "Better late than never, just like in the movies."

Thor was surrounded by two dozen assorted ranchers, police, and hands all firing question after question and demanding answers. It was Nate's two-fingered piercing whistle that stifled the commotion. "That's a darn sight better." He spat a stream of tobacco into a nearby bush. "Now, son, tell us all just what in tarnation happened. You and this here pilot," Nate pulled Hank close, "must have fought one helluva battle." He slapped Thor on the back. "Ya did a dandy job of ropin' and tyin' those varmints, boy."

"Cam did that," Hank interjected.

"How's that?" Nate choked on tobacco juice.

"Cam. She set up the whole thing. From a movie script we did last year. Blasted the Jeep and truck with harmless grenades and smoke bombs, then she and Devlin went one on one." Hank went on to elaborate. "Actually, Cam went five on one, tied those rustlers up neat as you please."

A murmur rippled through the all-male crowd but Nate was first to voice the question that tittered every man's tongue. "You tellin' us that it was the little lady who whopped and tied up those five big, strappin' men?"

"Sure," Hank answered. "Right, Devlin?"

Thor's affirmative nod was slow in coming.

"She's got a third- or fourth-degree black belt. Five to one odds are a piece of cake to her." His bald head turned left and right, eyes searching the crowd. "Say, where is she? Cam?"

Twenty-four men spread apart looking for the lone woman in their midst. She proved an easy find, sitting on the truck's loading ramp while examining her horse's front legs.

Totally absorbed in her work, it took Cam five minutes to realize that she was under scrutiny. She blinked at the men. They blinked back. She cleared her throat and said a simple "hi." When there was no immediate response, Cam added, "I suppose you'll be wanting a statement or something?"

The "or something" was provided by five of the rustlers. Handcuffed and groaning, they were prodded by state police officers toward the helicopter. As the thieves walked past the truck and spotted Cam, they shied together protectively. Their muttered phrases of "keep her away," "don't let her near," and "she tried to kill me" quelled every man's doubts as to who had shanghaied the rustlers.

One officer stopped and spoke quietly to Nate before herding the criminals away. The foreman winced, sniffed, and spat, but when he spoke his tone was respectful. "Seems this here little lady turned those mangy varmints from roosters to hens with five well-aimed kicks."

"It—it won't be permanent," she stammered. "I was just—"

"You just did one helluva job, ma'am," Nate held out his hand. "Boys! This calls for one big cel-e-bration. Grab the little lady and let's head home!" Ignoring her protesting squeals, Cam was hoisted on shoulders and paraded through the stomping, laughing masculine crowd.

When the dust settled, Thor was left standing all alone.

CHAPTER TEN

Mobile television news vans completely blocked Thor's house from view and the entire home pasture was filled with people. "What is all this?"

Nate grinned. "That repeater network works like a charm, son. Everyone within a hundred miles knows those dang rustlers are history." He slapped Thor on the back. "This will be a day to remember. Now, just where did our heroine disappear to? Oh, there she is, tyin' up her horse. Cam!"

The instant Nate shouted her name, Thor watched a human tidal wave crest. Cameras were shouldered, microphones extended, press photographers jockeyed for the best flash positions.

Thor took a deep breath and decided to join the milieu. "After all, I saw action. I knocked one of the rustlers out," he muttered to himself, trying to shoulder his way through the crowd.

But nobody noticed him. And an hour later, after the press had departed, Thor realized he hadn't been asked to answer a single question or pose for any pictures. Even the damn horse had had his photo taken.

Thor twisted the top off a bottle of beer, morose eyes reluctantly acknowledging the jubilant ranchers who partied around him. Only he was withdrawn, gloomy, and the lager that washed his tongue was bitter, biting.

As his hand wiped the taste from his mouth, he winced, his bruised, cut lip a hurtful reminder of his less-than-heroic encounter. Laughter focused Thor's attention on the real hero, Cam Stirling. Again she was front and center in the limelight.

Okay, okay, he silently rationalized, *so maybe she was being talked about rather than doing all the talking.* He listened to Hank Marsh's telling an enthralled audience story after story of her movie exploits.

Thor listened closely. Each tale became a brick and the bricks quickly turned into a wall, a wall that separated. Cam Stirling was no fragile camellia. *All right, all right, I knew she was no hothouse flower,* he mentally conceded.

Beauty. No doubting that. His eyes were witnesses to the radiant glow that bathed her comely features, his body hardening in immediate response to the sensual enticements only he had been privy to embrace.

Brains. More than that. She was witty, charming, clever, resourceful, and very self-sufficient. Very. And so full of life that it frightened him.

Brawn. Thor winced again. She was too alive, too athletic, too strong—what an understatement. *Hell, the woman is a weapon!* "And a better man than I am." His words came slow, their meaning harsh.

Thor Devlin was felled by the most fatal disease known to men—need, or, more accurately, the lack of being needed. He began to sweat. His heart beat against his ribs. The pounding exploded in his ears, in his throat, in his head.

He became a prisoner of his own distorted makings, shrinking into a dark corner on the front porch, completely oblivious to the laughter and festivities.

* * *

"Want to fly back to the camp with me?" Hank Marsh invited, stretching himself as he stood up from the lawn chair.

Cam shook her head. "No, I'm going to stay here. Help clean up." She exercised her wrist. "I think my fingers are broken."

"I know what you mean. We must have shook two hundred hands." He gave her a quick kiss on the cheek. "Okay, kid, be good. Don't do anything I wouldn't do." Hank winked. "That's not saying much."

"Where's Thor?" she asked Nate as they collected paper plates, cups, bottles, and cans into a large trash barrel. "You know, I don't think I've seen him in quite a while."

Nate shrugged. "Me either. Maybe he's givin' the police another statement. They sure asked enough questions." He shifted the chaw in his mouth. "Ya think we was the outlaws. I still like the old ways best. No questions asked, just hang 'em high."

Cam laughed. "I felt exactly like that when I learned Zodiac had been stolen." She leaned against the picnic table. "This is a terrible thing to say because I know your steers and equipment losses were in the millions but, well, those were nameless, faceless items to me. Not an animal that I raised, trained, and loved. I guess I went crazy."

"Lucky for us ya did. We're all gonna be able to really sleep tonight." Nate checked the area. "I'll have them boys bring some rakes up from the barn and finish this." He frowned. "Maybe Thor's in the house. I know the phone's been a-ringin'."

"I'll look inside. See you later." Cam picked up three empty beer bottles on the outside windowsill as she opened the back kitchen door. "Oh! Thor, here you are." She set the glass containers on the littered counter, checking under the sink for something to put more trash in.

"Well, it was certainly quite a day." Cam shook open a plastic garbage bag. "Could you believe all those reporters? And all the people. The food. I am tired. But it was fun."

"What was the funnest part?"

His surly tone made her stop cleaning. "I—I beg your pardon?"

"I said what was the funnest part?" He scraped the kitchen chair back, its wooden legs screeching along the tiles. "I can tell you what was fun for me—public humiliation."

Thor drew himself up to his full six foot four inches and squared his shoulders. "Did you enjoy doing that? Did you?" He stepped closer. "Oh, please, why the look of confusion? You weren't confused when you talked to the press. You weren't confused when you posed for pictures. You weren't confused when you signed autographs.

"You enjoyed being the hero, didn't you, Cam? Enjoyed being in control. Enjoyed showing off your superior strength. Wowing everyone with your kung fu prowess." His hands slashed the air. Then suddenly, Thor's eyes narrowed. "What are you staring at?"

"Not much."

"What kind of crack is that?"

"The truth." She expressed her feelings accurately and with no emotion. "Apparently, I had a better opinion of you than you deserve."

"What's that supposed to mean?"

Cam took a deep breath. "It means I thought I'd finally found a man who was not interested in a clichéd woman. I don't need a man to make me feel like something. I am something. I don't need to be claimed. I don't need to be controlled.

179

"I can walk, talk, think, act, love, laugh—I can do it all without asking permission. All women can. Most women do."

Her finger jabbed his chest. "You've got a distorted view, Devlin. A hero isn't a man who thinks with his fist. A hero thinks with his heart. A hero has an open mind. A hero knows the value of an equal." She jabbed him again. "I know exactly who and what I am. I thought you did too."

Thor pushed her hand away. "Oh, you're perfect."

Her smile was thin. "There's nothing wrong with me. You—you're the one who's got the growing up to do. You're the one who needs perfecting."

"Sure. I'm the bastard. I'm in the wrong."

"Yes. You are." Her blue eyes stared hard into his. "You were so damn worried about my being hurt. Well, worry no more, Luthor Devlin. I did get hurt. I fell in love with you." Cam elbowed him aside as she stalked to the door. "God help me, but the love's still there."

Abruptly, she turned and walked back. "No one meant to push you aside today. To leave you out. To embarrass you. And frankly, it only happened in your mind. And I could stick around and wait for you to see the funny side in all this. I could even tease you out of your sulk. But I'm not going to. I want to matter to your head and your heart. Not just your hormones." The slammed door was Cam Stirling's final rebuke.

Two minutes later, Nate stormed into the kitchen. "What in tarnation is goin' on around here? I heard the yellin'. Now, she's done takin' off on her horse." He looked Thor up and down. "And she said good-bye. Real final like."

Thor gestured expansively. "Hey, don't worry. She doesn't need you to worry about her. She doesn't need me. Hell, she doesn't need anyone or anything. She's a hero."

Nate bit the inside of his cheek instead of his wad of tobacco. "So that's it. You're jealous."

"I am not."

"You are too. I can read it on your face. Jealous and," he rubbed the gray stubble on his jaw, "spoiled. First your ma spoiled you. Then your pa. Then me. But she doesn't spoil ya, does she?"

"You don't know what you're talking about, Nate."

He grabbed Thor's arm. "The hell I don't, boy. You're a fool if you don't go after that gal."

"Fine. Then I'm a fool." When he tried pulling away, Nate's grip became tighter.

"If your pa was alive, he'd whop some sense into ya. But he ain't and I can't." Nate pushed him. "Na, I can't." He pushed him again. "I can't. Ah, the hell, I can't!"

Nate's fist connected a strong punch to Thor's jaw. "You're gonna end up kissin' your horse, boy." He hitched up his pants and slammed out of the kitchen, leaving Thor blinking in surprise over his bloody lip.

"Ya look like hell, boy."

"That's the first thing you've said to me in two days." Thor watched as Nate mounted the front porch steps. "Have a seat. Please."

He settled in the wooden rocker. "Figured ya stewed long enough. Feelin' different 'bout things?"

"Just more foolish." Thor extended his hand. "Thanks for hitting me."

Nate shook it. "Anytime." The two chairs rocked in unison. "Decide what you're gonna do?"

"Apologize."

"Nice afternoon for it."

Thor laughed, his thumb and forefinger massaging his mustache. "It's damn tough being a fool, especially where love is concerned."

181

"Ya weren't a fool about love, son," Nate returned kindly. "Just foolish with your pride. It ruled your head and controlled your heart."

"Never knew my ego was so fragile."

Nate pulled off a fresh plug of wintergreen tobacco, tucking it into his cheek. "Well, in that there area, I think I'm owed a punch." The foreman leaned sideways in the chair so his hand could rest on Thor's arm. "I'm owin' you an apology, son. I had no right to take over like I did. Seems like all that there Holl-e-wood glamour, what with the TeeVee cameras whirlin' and flashbulbs a-poppin', went right to my head.

"Ya know, boy, poor Cam just got drug along. I was pullin' at her. That there pilot, Hank, was runnin' off at the mouth 'bout her. Them press fellas grabbed into her. And all that poor gal was tryin' ta do was check out her horse!"

He scratched the gray stubble on his chin and sniffed. "What made matters worse was learnin' that those dang rustlers was from the East. Gol darn city slickers outfoxed us for months!" Nate relaxed back into the chair. "That was another reason why I put such a high gloss on the whole affair. Made us look more—"

"Tough?" came Thor's wry addendum.

"Yep."

"Unfortunately, I gave the tough one, the brave one, the woman I professed to love the short end of the deal." He ran a weary hand through his hair. "I felt even worse yesterday when I read the newspaper report. Cam sure spouted my name enough to those reporters."

Thor pushed out of the rocker. "I'm a bigger fool than even I care to admit, Nate. I fell in love with Cam Stirling for all the reasons I became jealous and afraid of her. And the only person I should have feared was myself." His head bowed. "She's a lot like my mother,

Nate. Same courage, same toughness, same temperament, and so easy to fall in love with."

"Don't tell me, boy, go tell her."

"An excellent idea." Thor adjusted the brim on his black Stetson. "I'll go saddle up and—"

"All ready done," Nate grinned. He jerked his thumb toward the barn. "Vamoose, boy, sundown's comin' and that's the prettiest time of day for smoochin'."

Thor galloped back to the ranch four hours later with a lathered horse and an agitated disposition. "They're gone."

Nate dropped the curb bit he'd been repairing. "What d'ya mean, she's gone?"

He used his shirt sleeve to mop the sweat from his eyes, his massive chest heaving. "Not just Cam, Nate. Everyone. The entire movie company. Lock, stock, barrel, cameras, elephant, tiger—all of it gone. I checked at the ranger station and was told they packed up yesterday." Thor braced his body against a fence post for support. "Now what am I going to do?"

"Find her." Nate slapped his shoulder. "Cal-e-forn-ya may be on another planet to me but it ain't for you."

Thor straightened up, smiling. "You're right. You're damn right. Hell, I spent six months in L.A. as a consulting engineer. I can get around all right." Thor massaged the back of his neck as he paced back and forth. "Okay, okay, ah, well, we've got to bring the Fresh Air kids to the bus station at seven tomorrow morning and then I'll head to the airport."

Nate grabbed the stallion's reins. "The hands and I can handle things here. Nothin' much doin' now anyways." A grin ripped his lean features as he yelled to Thor's departing figure, "Hey, find out if I can borrow John Wayne's belt for the weddin'!"

The little isolated triangle of mountains and valley was a sliver of old California, when the West was young and wild. It took Thor twenty minutes to reach the crest of the San Marcos Pass. Below was the lush panorama of the Santa Ynez Valley with the rugged Sierra Madre Mountains shimmering beyond. The view was both majestic and peaceful—which was more than you could say for the road.

The precision-graded highway abruptly became a rock-strewn drive that could easily pass for an endless Montana cattle trail. A mailbox was stenciled STIRLING, and on the post was a sign proclaiming: DON'T GIVE UP—and Thor Devlin intended to follow its advice to the letter.

Thor blessed his choice of a four-wheel-drive rental with every bone-jarring foot. According to his map, it was a simple trek. Apparently the mapmakers had never navigated this rutted stretch. He bumped and jounced his way, the speedometer registering less than ten miles an hour as he fought the steering with each twist and turn.

The tires gripped smooth concrete the same instant his eyes sighted a weathered barn. Thor's muscles relaxed, his grim expression transforming into a smile. A second later, his happiness became a horror when a body smashed into the front fender of his Jeep and somersaulted across the hood.

"Oh, my God!" Thor hit the brakes hard, his seat belt holding him firmly in place despite the natural whiplash action. Releasing the shoulder harness, he scrambled out of the car.

A small elderly woman, shopping bag still clutched in her hand, lay in a heap by the oversized tire. Thor stared from his own shaking fingers to her body, his mind whirling in a dozen directions.

Knowing enough not to move her, Thor bent to check her pulse, shedding his suit jacket at the same time to use as a blanket. A voice halted his actions.

"She won't be needing that, mister. Maggie! You've scared the man half out of his wits. Get up!"

Thor found himself being scrutinized by a pair of twinkling brown eyes. "Sorry. Thought you were family." An impish smile set the woman's face in motion. "Don't you dare help me up, young man." She slapped his hand away and, with a supple grace, bounded to her feet. "Seems we've got company, Ruth. Well, do you speak English, mister, or just blink at people?"

"I—I thought you were dead."

"Good. I was supposed to look dead." Her fingers fluffed the yellow-gray waves that framed fragile features. "Hear that, Ruth? Told you the tumbling would cinch it."

"And you were right," Ruth agreed, stepping from behind a large hedge. "You looked real good from this angle too." Her blue gaze examined Thor. "Oh, you're getting your color back. Thought you were going to faint on us for a minute."

Thor watched Ruth whisper into Maggie's ear, then both women turned beaming smiles in his direction. "You're Cam's grandmothers."

"And you're that Devlin fellow," Maggie stated. "What took you so long to get here?"

"Maggie!" Ruth elbowed her ribs.

"Don't do that!" She stepped closer to Thor. "Besides, I'm old enough that I can get away with saying anything I want." Her eyebrow lifted. "I like your grin, Devlin."

"And I love your granddaughter."

"Good."

"Where is she?"

185

Maggie cleared her throat. "Cam's resting quite comfortably in room 423 at Cottage Hospital."

"Oh, dear, he's gone pale again," Ruth patted Thor's arm. "Nothing to worry about, honey, seeing you will help Cam mend. Give the man directions, Maggie, you're so much better at telling people where to go than I am."

Thor stood outside room 423 and tried to erase the fact that this was a hospital and Cam Stirling was inside. Her condition couldn't be that critical, he rationalized. After all, her grandmothers weren't concerned. In fact, they were giggling and waving as he drove away.

He took a deep breath, his nose twitching from the sterile atmosphere, and pushed open the door. The private room was cool and dark. Thin strands of daylight waved down the window blinds, casting a silvery umbra on a sleeping feminine form.

"Cam . . ." Thor's hand hovered just above her forehead, the tips of his fingers dancing against the silken tumble of platinum bangs. His knuckles tenderly caressed her cheek, her skin feeling soft and smooth to his touch. "Cam . . ."

She moaned, turning toward his voice and caress. Her lashes fluttered, eyes blinking rapidly, opening wide, then closing, as if in disbelief. Husky words echoed sweetly in her ear.

"An old Chinese proverb says 'all man's mistakes fly out of his mouth'." Thor smiled into her eyes. "You know the love of a good woman reformed my great-great-grandfather. Worked the same for me."

"And have you reformed?" came her polite inquiry.

"I recognized that I was a pompous, stubborn, spoiled, jealous, prideful—whoops!"

Cam grabbed a handful of his shirt and pulled him

186

down on the bed. "I won't have you talking about the man I love that way."

He pressed a hard kiss to her lips. "Hmm, I'm so glad to hear you say that word. Love. Because I love you too much to lose you." Thor's arms wrapped around her, his tone quite fierce. "Your work made you who you are. And I fell in love with who you are. Whatever it takes to make this relationship work, we'll do it," he said.

"I love you that much. I know what pleasure your work brings to you and that brings pleasure to me. I don't know how we're going to make it work. I don't have a master plan. But I feel we can do it." He hugged her tight, loving the way her body intuitively conformed against his. "I know I can handle anything as long as you're by my side."

Her fingertips pressed into the rugged planes and angles of his face. "I've missed you. The days and nights were long and lonely."

He nuzzled her neck, the haunting smell of jasmine and roses heightening his senses. "Hmm, I couldn't stop thinking about you. And when I thought about you, I knew I couldn't lose the one important thing that ever entered my life."

"How long did that revelation take to hit, Mr. Devlin?" She teased.

"Twenty-four hours, Miss Stirling, but you were gone." Thor frowned. "What happened?"

"Oh, Bridget filed a complaint with the Directors Guild and came back to Hollywood. Things limped along, tensions were increasing, everyone was arguing. So Jack shut everything down and before I could blink, I was back here."

His hand pressed along her body. "Where are you hurt?"

"Hurt?"

"Your grandmother said you were resting comfortably."

Cam laughed. "I'm taking a nap. I spent the last nine hours being a labor coach to a stunt woman friend. Her husband was on location in Yugoslavia, so I subbed. She did all the work, but I was too exhausted to drive home. The head nurse let me sleep in here."

Her fingernail outlined his lips. "You know, you just had that same cute, horrified expression slide across your face that you had in the ladies' room at the pizza parlor."

Thor nipped at her finger. "And you're blushing as brightly now as you did then. Going to let me in on the secret?"

She snuggled tight against him, her arms looping his neck, her face buried in the curve of his shoulder. "Oh, it's silly, but I can just imagine that look on your son's face—our son's face," Cam shyly corrected, "when he heard his pet snake ended up in the washer."

He tipped her face up. "That has a lovely ring to it. But I'm going to insist we have more than one. No more spoiled only children with the Devlin brand."

"Sounds good to me."

"What are you doing?"

"Unbuttoning your shirt." She kissed his chest. "Next your pants. Please, get rid of those boots."

"This is a hospital room."

"I know," she whispered back, fumbling with his zipper, "but they promised I wouldn't be disturbed for three hours. And it seems to me, I was just being compared to a Chinese menu when we were rudely interrupted."

"So you were."

Cam smiled as his boots hit the floor. "Let's see. One from column A, or was it two from column A?"

"You definitely need a refresher course," Thor murmured before his mouth reunited with hers.

Now you can reserve May's

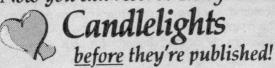

Candlelights

<u>before</u> they're published!

♥ You'll have copies set aside for *you*
    the instant they come off press.
♥ You'll save yourself precious shopping
    time by arranging for *home delivery.*
♥ You'll feel proud and efficient about
    organizing a system that *guarantees* delivery.
♥ You'll avoid the disappointment of not
    finding *every* title you want and need.

ECSTASY SUPREMES $2.75 each

☐ **169 NIGHT OF THE MATADOR**, Lee Magner 16397-8
☐ **170 CAPTURED BY A COWBOY**, Becky Barker . . 10963-9
☐ **171 A SECRET ARRANGEMENT**, Linda Vail 17672-7
☐ **172 DANGEROUS HIDEAWAY**, Kit Daley 11678-3

ECSTASY ROMANCES $2.25 each

☐ **504 FIRST-CLASS MALE**, Donna Kimel Vitek 12554-5
☐ **505 ONCE UPON A DREAM**, JoAnn Stacey 16722-1
☐ **506 MISCHIEF-MAKER**, Molly Katz 15572-X
☐ **507 FANCY FOOTWORK**, Cory Kenyon 12445-X
☐ **508 A LOVER'S MYSTIQUE**, Eleanor Woods 15032-9
☐ **509 ARIEL'S DESIRE**, Aimee Thurlo 10322-3
☐ **8 OCEAN OF REGRETS**, Noelle Berry McCue . . 16592-X
☐ **23 RIGHT OF POSSESSION**, Jayne Castle 17441-4

 At your local bookstore or use this handy coupon for ordering:

DELL READERS SERVICE—DEPT. B1465A
6 REGENT ST., LIVINGSTON, N.J. 07039

Please send me the above title(s) I am enclosing $ _____ (please add 75¢ per copy to cover
postage and handling) Send check or money order—no cash or CODs Please allow 3-4 weeks for shipment

Ms /Mrs /Mr _____

Address _____

City/State _____ Zip _____

Wisconsin Indianhead Technical Institute
2100 Beaser
Ashland, WI 54806